THE
CO-CO'S

★ "A charming debut about a thoughtful, creative preteen connecting to both halves of her identity."
—***KIRKUS REVIEWS***, starred review

★ "Those who enjoy vivacious, plucky heroines . . . will eagerly embrace Malú." —***SCHOOL LIBRARY JOURNAL***, starred review

★ "Pérez's debut is as exuberant as its heroine . . . A rowdy reminder that people are at their best when they aren't forced into neat, tidy boxes." —***PUBLISHERS WEEKLY***, starred review

"Pérez draws heavily on the intersections of community that are integral to Mexican-American culture . . . It is this element that makes Malú's obvious growth by the end of the book so rewarding." —***BCCB***

A PURA BELPRÉ AUTHOR HONOR BOOK ϟ AN ALSC NOTABLE CHILDREN'S BOOK ϟ A TOMÁS RIVERA MEXICAN AMERICAN CHILDREN'S BOOK AWARD WINNER ϟ AN ABA INDIES INTRODUCE TITLE ϟ A KIDS' INDIE NEXT LIST PICK ϟ AN E.B. WHITE READ-ALOUD MIDDLE READER HONOR BOOK ϟ AN AMELIA BLOOMER LIST BOOK ϟ A CCBC CHOICES TITLE ϟ A BANK STREET BEST CHILDREN'S BOOK OF THE YEAR ϟ A JUNIOR LIBRARY GUILD SELECTION ϟ A *PUBLISHERS WEEKLY* FLYING START ϟ AN NPR BEST BOOK OF THE YEAR ϟ A *KIRKUS REVIEWS* BEST BOOK OF THE YEAR ϟ A *SCHOOL LIBRARY JOURNAL* BEST BOOK OF THE YEAR ϟ A *HORN BOOK* FANFARE SELECTION ϟ A CENTER FOR THE STUDY OF MULTICULTURAL CHILDREN'S LITERATURE BEST BOOK OF THE YEAR ϟ A DOROTHY CANFIELD FISHER CHILDREN'S BOOK AWARD NOMINEE ϟ A SUNSHINE STATE YOUNG READERS AWARD NOMINEE ϟ A NERDY BOOK AWARD WINNER

EVENT CODE
SECTION/AISLE
GENADM
ROW/BOX
1011
SEAT
1032
ADMISS
CONVENIENCE CHARGE
$ 6.00
$ 1.50
GENERAL ADMISSN
MASQUERADE CONCERTS PRES
ALL AGES WELCOME
THE MASQUERADE
1503 E 7TH AVE-YBOR CITY
GENADM
2X
CA
0111032
OQT1550
N11DEC9
COMETB
$2
#34
frida ♥ diego
mailorder
Big Cheese
¡mamasita!
EL

OTHER BOOKS YOU MAY ENJOY

Counting by 7s	Holly Goldberg Sloan
The Epic Fail of Arturo Zamora	Pablo Cartaya
Fish in a Tree	Lynda Mullaly Hunt
The Great Treehouse War	Lisa Graff
One for the Murphys	Lynda Mullaly Hunt
Short	Holly Goldberg Sloan
Three Times Lucky	Sheila Turnage
Well, That Was Awkward	Rachel Vail

THE FIRST RULE OF PUNK

CELIA C. PÉREZ

PUFFIN BOOKS

PUFFIN BOOKS
An imprint of Penguin Random House LLC
375 Hudson Street
New York, New York 10014

First published in the United States of America by Viking, an imprint of Penguin Random House LLC, 2017
Published by Puffin Books, an imprint of Penguin Random House LLC, 2018

LIBRARY OF CONGRESS CATALOGING-IN-PUBLICATION DATA
Names: Pérez, Celia C., author.
Title: The first rule of punk / by Celia C. Pérez.
Description: New York : Viking, [2017] | Summary: Twelve-year-old María Luisa O'Neill-Morales (who really prefers to be called Malú) reluctantly moves with her Mexican-American mother to Chicago and starts seventh grade with a bang—violating the dress code with her punk rock aesthetic and spurning the middle school's most popular girl in favor of starting a band with a group of like-minded weirdos.
Identifiers: LCCN 2017010474 | ISBN 9780425290408 (hardback)
Subjects: | CYAC: Individuality—Fiction. | Friendship—Fiction. | Mexican Americans—Fiction. | Punk rock music—Fiction. | Bands (Music)—Fiction. | Middle schools—Fiction. | Schools—Fiction. | Chicago (Ill.)—Fiction. | BISAC: JUVENILE FICTION/ People & Places/ United States/ Hispanic & Latino. | JUVENILE FICTION/ Performing Arts/ Music. | JUVENILE FICTION/ Social Issues / Friendship. Classification: LCC PZ7.1.P44747 Fi 2017 | DDC [Fic]—dc23 LC record available at https://lccn.loc.gov/2017010474

Puffin Books ISBN 9780425290422

Printed in U.S.A. Set in Archer Book design by Kate Renner

10 9 8

For Emiliano, for my mom, Gloria,

AND

In memory of my sister, Gloria A. Tuñon
1970–2012

Chapter 1

Dad says punk rock only comes in one volume: loud. So when I slipped my headphones over my ears, I turned the music up until bass strings thumped, cymbals hissed, and guitar strings squealed like they were having a conversation with each other. Mom says my music is a racket, but to me it's like the theme music to my life. And it's always helped me concentrate.

I ripped a page out of a magazine, then squeezed my fingers inside the blue plastic holes of an old pair of school scissors. It was a little too close for comfort, but my real scissors, the ones made of steel with a black handle, were packed away, and I had to get this done. It was now or never.

I maneuvered the blades carefully around the page. I liked the feeling of the scissors slicing through the glossy paper. Especially when I got to the very last snip and freed the exact piece I wanted. The word I cut out stuck to my sweaty fingertips, and I carefully placed it on the floor, where my zine supplies were spread out around me.

There were sheets of unlined paper and old magazines Dad had given me, an uncapped purple glue stick, and a folder so fat with clip art that papers spilled out of the opening. The yellow Whitman's Sampler box that held my colored pencils, stickers, and scraps of paper still smelled of chocolate but no longer contained a delicious assortment of candy.

While hunched over the magazine, looking for more letters to cut out, a pair of leather-sandaled feet suddenly appeared. I looked up at Mom, who stood over me in her HECHO EN MEXICO T-shirt and a knee-length gauzy skirt. Her lips moved, but her words were no match for my music. Finally she pointed to her ears.

"SuperMexican strikes again," I said, pulling the headphones down around my neck.

SuperMexican is my nickname for Mom. She's always trying to school me on stuff about Mexico and Mexican American people. I think her main goal in life is to make me into her ideal Mexican American señorita. Plus, she likes to wear these embroidered dresses and skirts, and wraps called rebozos. I call this her SuperMexican uniform. Mom acts like it annoys her, but I think she secretly likes the nickname.

"Funny," Mom said. "You all done packing?"

"I guess." I glanced over at the pile of boxes and bags next to the door.

Mom told me to bring everything I needed but not to overpack, which didn't make any sense. My room wasn't my room without my things. There were only a few belongings I decided to leave behind, and they became the only signs that I'd ever lived here. I felt like someone had taken a giant Pink Pearl eraser and rubbed me out of the picture.

"Great," Mom said. "Your dad will be here in an hour, so get ready."

"I *am* ready." I looked down at my T-shirt and shorts.

Mom's eyes moved over my clothes with their super-scanning powers, looking for holes, stains, and other un-señorita-like offenses to point out. But before she could comment on anything, she noticed the magazine I was cutting.

"Malú, that's not my new magazine that just came in the mail, is it?"

I gave Mom an unapologetic smirk to let her know that it was.

"I'll take that, thank you very much," she said, holding out her hand. "If you need magazines, check the recycling bin."

"Yes, ma'am," I said, and saluted before I handed her the copy of *Bon Appétit*.

I put my headphones back on and grabbed a blank sheet of paper. I had to get this zine done before Dad came to pick me up.

I started making zines earlier this year when I discovered Dad's collection of punk music zines from his high school days. Zines are self-published booklets, like home-made magazines, and they can be about anything—not just punk. There are zines about all kinds of topics, like video games and candy and skateboarding. A zine can be a tribute to someone or something you love and nerd out about or a place to share ideas and opinions. Dad said they're also a good way to write about what you're thinking or feeling, kind of like a diary that you share with people. Mine are mostly about stuff I find interesting or want to know more about. But ever since Mom told me we were moving, a lot of my zines had become about that.

Mom made it seem like this move was no big deal because we'd be back when her new job contract expired. But two years might as well be forever. Two years meant all of middle school. And I couldn't even imagine what two years away from Dad would feel like. It was a *very* big deal. So for the next hour I wrote and cut and pasted a final plea to Mom. I glued the last letter onto a page just as the doorbell rang to signal that my time was up.

there is no place like

HOME IS DAD & MARTÍ

Martí the poet (not him!)

Martí the cute dog (him!)

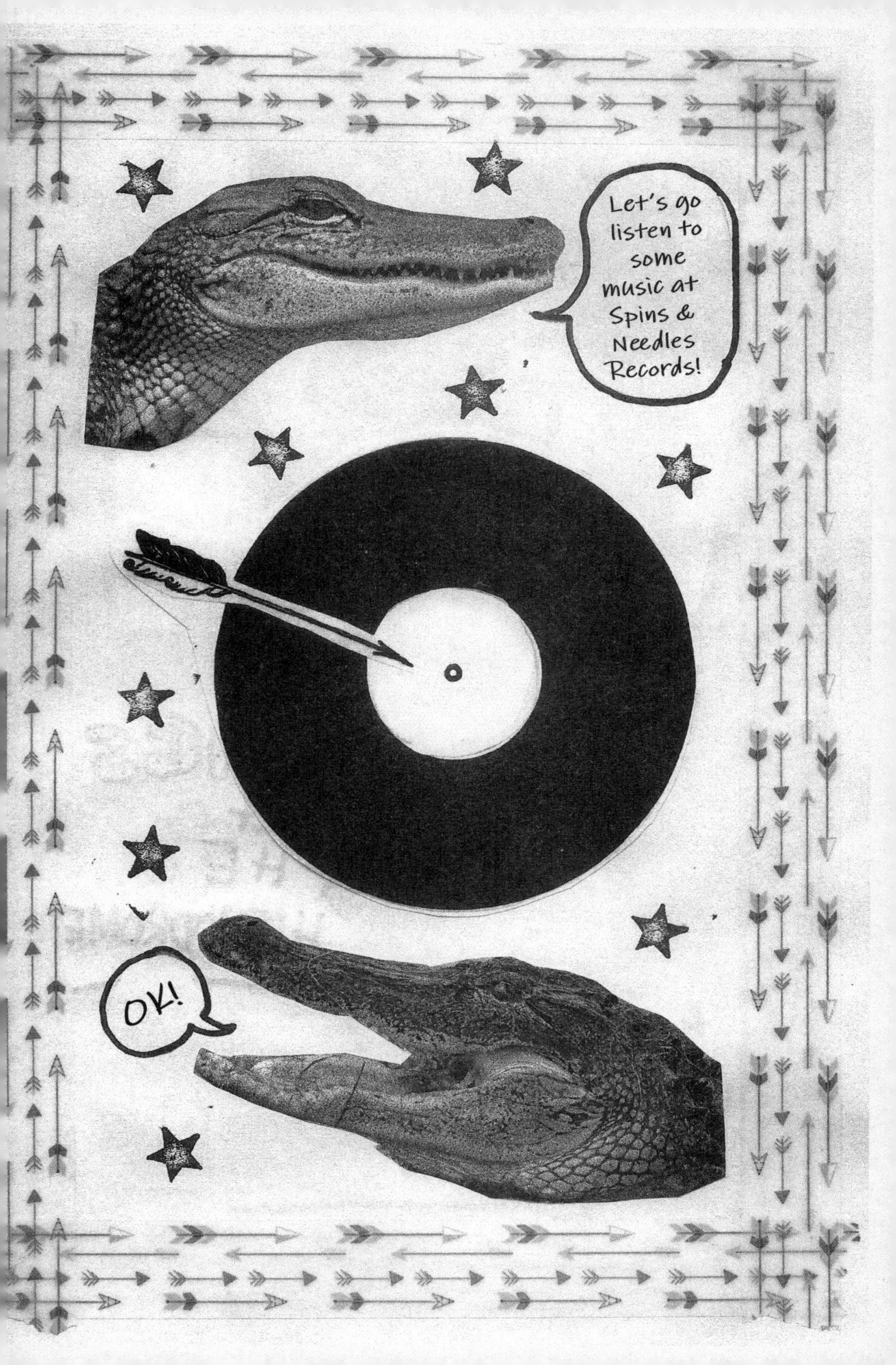
Let's go listen to some music at Spins & Needles Records!
OK!

UNCHAINED BOOKS
books, not a graph
bookstore cat
Movies
at
The Hippodrome
RESERVED
ROW
SEAT
B
G
15
ADMIT ONE THIS DATE
NOV
1
HIPPODROM
902534
ADMIT ONE
38032286
Rogers

SKaTiNg

(or trying to!) outside the ART building on campus

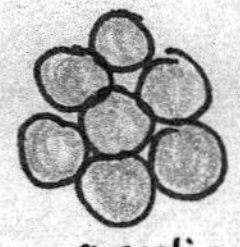

+

+

garlic butter rolls!

spinach and tomato pizza!

root beer!

Friday night dinner with Dad at

Spanish moss
hanging from trees
like ghosts.
10
EL ARBOL
Afternoon thunderstorms.

When the delivery guy throws our bag of bagels onto the porch from his bike. THUD! And . . .

bagels bagels everywhere!

love

COMFORT

family

roots

fun

HEART

CALM

HAPPY

SAFE

HOME

Chapter 2

When I walked into the living room, Mom was sitting on the couch, talking to Dad, her knitting bag next to her. The coiled scarf on her lap grew as her wooden needles clicked and clacked under and over and through the yarn. It was a hideous rainbow of pastels, like the tentacle of a Lucky Charms–colored sea monster. I scowled at the scarf and slipped the zine into Mom's bag before throwing my arms around Dad.

"Lú!"

Dad scooped me up in a bear hug.

"Hmm, a gift for me?" Mom asked, glancing at the zine.

I nodded and straightened my T-shirt as Dad put me down.

"Malú, do you think you could wear something a little nicer?" Mom asked. "This is your last dinner with your dad for a while. It would be so lovely to see you looking like una señorita. I'd even settle for a fresh T-shirt."

"She's fine," Dad said.

"See, Mom?" I grinned as obnoxiously as I could at her.

"Of course," Mom said, looking from me to Dad. "Peas in a pod."

She was right. Dad wore his usual ratty black Chuck Taylors, a black Spins & Needles Records T-shirt, and cutoff corduroys. I had on my Doc Marten boots, a black Ramones T-shirt, and cutoff khakis. Dad and I looked at each other and laughed.

"We're twinsies," I said.

"Really, it's no big deal, Magaly," Dad said. "We're just getting takeout and hanging out at the store."

"Come on, Dad." I grabbed his arm and pulled.

"Fine, have a good night," Mom said. "And don't forget our flight is at noon, Michael."

"I'll be here with my chariot," Dad said as he closed the door behind him.

We wheeled our bikes out of the yard, and Dad handed me my helmet.

"I hate that scarf," I said through gritted teeth.

"Scarf?"

"Mom's never-ending knitting project. It's a bad omen."

Dad laughed. "I didn't know you were so superstitious," he said.

"I'm serious, Dad. That scarf only appears when Mom's stressed about something." I snapped the chin-strap buckle of my bike helmet. "She was knitting all the time before she told me we were moving. Coincidence? I don't think so."

"Well, how about we forget the evil scarf for now?" Dad said. "We have some DaVinci's to pick up. I ordered all your favorites."

"Awesome," I said. "Because right now it feels like I'll never have DaVinci's again."

My mouth watered thinking about the food as we rode our bikes the few blocks to our once-a-week dinner spot. If I had to have a last meal on my final night at home, I wanted it to be DaVinci's with Dad.

After we picked up our food, we rode back to Dad's place, stopping under the sign that hung over the entrance to his store. The sign looked and spun like a real vinyl record. In the middle the SPINS & NEEDLES logo went around and around.

When Dad opened the door, Martí, his pit bull, ran out to greet us. Dad was funny about Martí's name, always making sure people knew how to pronounce it properly.

"It's Mar-TEE, like José Martí the Cuban poet, not MAR-tee like Marty McFly from *Back to the Future*." Most times people would look at him like they had no idea what he was talking about.

After today I wouldn't see Martí run through the door or hear Dad correct people's pronunciation. Two more things to say good-bye to.

"What's happening, buddy?" I asked, scratching Martí behind the ears. He wagged his tail and sniffed at me until he realized Dad had the food, then trotted off after him.

"Traitor," I said, shaking my head.

"What do you want to listen to?" Dad asked from behind the counter.

"You pick it."

"You know they've got some great record stores in Chicago," Dad said. "You'll have to check out Laurie's Planet of Sound."

"That's great," I said. "But it doesn't matter because none of them will be *this* place."

Spins & Needles wasn't just a record store; it was my second home. Dad had owned it for as long as I could remember. He lived in the apartment upstairs. When I was sick and stayed home from school at his place, he would play quiet, soothing music because he knew the sound traveled upstairs easily.

I loved spending time with Dad at the store, listening to records. My favorite stuff was from the seventies and eighties, old punk that Dad always played. I helped him around the store too. I made sure the records were alphabetized in their correct bins, and I decorated the white plastic separators between bands.

But the best thing was being there when people crowded in to watch a band. The air would hang warm and heavy, and sometimes there wouldn't even be room to pogo because the store would get so packed. The energy of the band and the crowd made me feel like there were hyper butterflies trapped inside me. The music would flow through the store like a magic carpet inviting me to hop on for a ride. You could stand so close to a band, it was like you were part of them. Some bands even welcomed people to sing along into the microphone. I always wanted to sing, but I never did because I was too scared.

"How'd you know I was in a Smiths mood, Dad?" I asked when the store's sound system crackled to life.

The song started out with a jangly, quiet guitar and a voice that sounded sad but a little hopeful, too. Like when you're stuck inside on a rainy Sunday and all you really want is for the sun to peek out so that you might be able to go outside, even for just a little while, before the school week begins.

"Just a lucky guess. Shall we dance?"

Dad grabbed one of my hands in his and put his other arm around my waist. I couldn't stop giggling as he waltzed me around the record store and sang along. The song was about someone with crummy luck. I knew the feeling, so I joined in at the chorus, begging to get what I wanted for once.

Dad twirled me toward the counter and let go of my hand.

"Thanks for the dance, kid," he said. "Now let me get some plates so we can eat."

I gave Dad a thumbs-up and turned to the record bin labeled NEW (USED) ARRIVALS. I pulled out a record by a band I recognized and studied the singer's face on the cover. The singer seemed to stare back, her hair teased and standing on end. She had her signature dark, heavily made-up eyes and lips. It was a look that made her a little scary, like an angry witch, but also kind of pretty. This reminded me of Mom and how she called punk music "a racket." It always bummed me out that she could hear the anger but not the beauty in it like I did.

"I bet I could do that to my hair no problem," I said. "What do you think, Dad?"

I held up the album cover for him to see.

"Sure," Dad said, digging through a drawer for utensils.

"So you think it would be okay for me to do it?" I asked hopefully.

"You definitely have to ask your mom about that."

"That's not fair," I said. "She's making me move across the country. Can I *at least* decide how I look?"

"You're entitled to feel that way, Lú," Dad said, handing me a paper plate and a napkin. "But you still have to talk to your mom."

"Sometimes I wish you two argued like normal divorced parents," I mumbled.

"No, you don't," Dad said.

"Yeah, you're right."

I knew I was lucky. I liked that my parents got along even though they weren't together. People always assumed my mom and dad were like other divorced parents, who fought over everything, but they were actually friends. They split up when I was a baby, so I had no memories, just some old photos.

"Anyway, she doesn't like how I dress, so what's one more thing?"

"Mom doesn't dislike the way you dress," Dad said.

"Nice verbal gymnastics, Dad."

"Really, she's used to wacky outfits and loud music. She was married to me, wasn't she?"

"No comment." I grabbed a roll and stuffed the whole thing into my mouth.

"I think you and your mom are more alike than you realize."

"SuperMexican and I are nothing alike," I said through bread.

"You both do that scrunchy thing with your upper lip and nose." He laughed just thinking about it.

"This is serious, Dad."

"I know. I'm sorry."

"I still don't understand why I can't stay with you."

"I knew this was coming," Dad said. The look on his face told me he didn't want to have this conversation. "Malú, you know my schedule is too unpredictable. That's why you live with your mom, remember?"

"But I'm almost thirteen," I said. "And very responsible. You know that!"

"True," Dad said. "But this is a done deal."

I could feel my hope crumbling as if one of those huge wrecking balls used to tear down buildings had just slammed against it, turning it into dust. I thought of the zine I'd left for Mom.

"What if Mom changes her mind tonight?"

Dad gave me a look like he was questioning my grip on reality.

"She could," I said indignantly. "Parents don't always know best, you know."

"Can't argue with that," Dad said.

I emptied my root beer can into a plastic cup and watched the foam threaten to spill over.

"Look, think of it as your big city adventure," Dad said. "How many kids get to be in a new and exciting place for a while and then come back home?"

"Yeah, I must be the luckiest kid in the world."

Dad opened the pizza box, and the warm smell of baked crust and melted cheese rose up, but my appetite had disappeared. Talking about moving had ruined my last DaVinci's.

"Sorry, kid," Dad said. "This is going to be hard for all of us, but we'll get through it, right?"

Neither Mom nor Dad seemed especially torn up about it, to be honest. I could feel my eyes well up with tears, but I didn't want to cry. So I grabbed a slice of pizza and busied myself by picking at the tomatoes and rearranging them into an angry face.

"Let's not spend our last night together feeling sad," Dad said. "Here, I got you a little gift."

He pulled a small shoe box from behind the counter and placed it in front of me.

"A gift isn't going to make me feel better," I said. "But can I open it now?" I gave Dad a sheepish grin.

"Of course," he said.

I pulled off the lid and picked up the small, oval-shaped yellow box that sat on top. It was so light, it felt empty. Inside were six tiny dolls that looked like stick figures, with ink dots for eyes and mouths. Each doll was about as big as my thumbnail, with cardboard limbs wrapped in colorful thread made to look like clothes.

"What are they?" I asked, carefully tapping the dolls out onto the counter.

"Worry dolls," Dad said. "You put them under your pillow when you go to bed, tell them your worries, and they take them away while you sleep."

"Do they really work?" I asked.

"You'll have to tell me," Dad said. "I thought they might come in handy."

I nodded and scooped the dolls back into their tiny container. The other item in the shoe box was Dad's old Walkman cassette player and a cassette in its plastic case.

"Cool! You made me a mix?"

"I put some new stuff and some old stuff on there," Dad said. "I hope you like it."

"Is the Walkman a gift too?" I asked, hopefully.

"How about I let you borrow it?" Dad said. "Return it when you're back home again."

I threw my arms around Dad and kissed his cheek.

"You may be far from home, kid, but you can take the music anywhere," Dad said. "It's always with you."

"Thanks, Dad."

"Hey, you want to play DJ?"

"Sure," I said, and hopped off my stool.

Normally I loved playing DJ at the record store, but for once it wasn't getting me out of my sad mood. Still, I pulled some of our favorites to play over the store's speakers while we finished eating.

After dinner we cleaned up and took photos in the old photo booth, one strip for each of us. I looked around the store one last time, pretending my eyes were a camera, and snapped mental shots to tuck away for safekeeping. Then I turned off the lights.

Upstairs, Dad put on *The Wizard of Oz* while I changed into my pajamas. It was one of my favorite movies, and watching it together once a year had become our thing. I squeezed in between Dad and Martí on the couch. I always loved the beginning, where Dorothy's in Kansas and everything is a brownish gray.

"Don't listen to this part," I said to Martí, covering his ears when Miss Gulch threatened to harm Toto.

I knew I was too old, but I snuggled close to Dad anyway and breathed deep into his shirt, trying to memorize his familiar smell of laundry detergent, peppermint gum, and sweat. I wondered when we'd be able to watch the movie together again.

"Dad?" I said, hesitating. I felt like a water balloon about to burst.

"Lú?"

"I know it's not punk to be scared . . . but I'm scared."

"It's okay to be scared, Lú." Dad squeezed my hand. "Hey, do you remember what the first rule of punk is?"

"There are no rules?" I asked.

"Okay, never mind," he said, and laughed. "The second rule of punk?"

"The louder, the better?"

"You're a real comedian."

"I know, I know," I said. "Be myself." I'd heard Dad say the same thing five thousand times. "But how's that supposed to help me?"

"Well, it'll help you make new friends, find your people."

"I have friends," I said, before I could stop myself. "I don't want new friends."

Dad didn't respond, but I knew what he was thinking. It was the same thing I was thinking. I didn't really have any close friends at school. I considered Dad my people more than anyone else. I guess Mom was my people too, though she was different from Dad and me. It looked like I had a lot of people finding to do.

"I know," Dad said, and nudged his chin toward the screen. "But you're going to need a Yellow-Brick-Road posse." He squeezed me tight and kissed the top of my head.

Dad kept telling me not to worry. That everything was going to be okay. I really wanted to believe him. But as I watched Dorothy's house fly up into the air and spin around in the twister, I wasn't so sure.

Chapter 3

"Welcome home," Mom said, unlocking the door and dropping our bags at her feet.

"This isn't home," I mumbled under my breath.

The mat that was spread out in front of the doorway insisted otherwise. It read: HOME SWEET HOME. I did my best to avoid stepping on it and followed Mom down a long hallway.

"Well, it's home for now," she said, poking her head into each of the doorways. "It's a little plain, but we'll make it homey, right?"

"Sure, Martha Stewart," I said. "But you know what else is homey? Our *real* home."

"Malú, why don't you go pick out your room?" Mom said, ignoring my snarky comment.

I leaned my suitcase against a kitchen wall and sat down on it, arms crossed.

"Come on," Mom said. "You're acting like a baby."

"Am not."

"You don't want first dibs on rooms? Suit yourself."

"Fine. I'll go," I said, getting up.

"I'm going to do some unpacking," she said. "We can take a walk in a little while, check out the neighborhood."

I grabbed my bags and wandered back down the hallway. We were supposed to live on campus in family housing, where other faculty and students lived with their families, but there were no apartments available, so someone in the English department helped Mom find this place. It was furnished in that generic way homes in furniture catalogs are. Nothing too personal or too bright or too different that might make it stand out in any way. Definitely no turquoise-colored walls like back home. Who would ever want to live in a furniture catalog photo?

One bedroom was bigger, but the smaller one had more windows, so that's where I dropped my stuff. The bare walls were painted a pale green that reminded me of the hospital room where I recovered after I had my appendix taken out.

Looking around my new bedroom, I felt a tightness in my chest, like I couldn't breathe. I pictured my heart and ribs blown from glass, tiny air bubbles throughout, like in the documentary about Mexican glassblowers I'd watched with Mom that summer. It felt like something was pressing down on me and my glass insides were going to crack into a million pieces.

I couldn't stand looking at the empty walls, so I opened my backpack and took out my folder of pictures and articles I had up on the walls of my room back home. Most images were of my favorite bands, stuff I'd torn out of magazines or printed from the Internet. I tacked up my favorite picture of Poly Styrene of the X-Ray Spex in her sausage-and-eggs dress, and Frida Kahlo on the cover of Mexican *Vogue*. The last thing I put up was the photo booth strip of me and Dad at Spins & Needles.

When I was done, I pulled out my zine supplies and a sheet of paper that I folded into eighths.

"Good choice," Mom said, appearing in the doorway. "We can paint if you want. Maybe get some curtains?"

"Sure," I said, tucking the papers inside a book.

"You hungry?"

"Not really," I said. "I think there might be a bowling ball sitting in my stomach."

"A bowling ball, huh?"

"And it's not one of the small ones for little hands, either," I said. "It's the biggest size, like the ones Dad uses."

"Sounds bad," Mom said. "Why don't you try to walk it off? You don't have to eat, but I think you'll feel better."

"Can I just stay here and work on this?"

"You can't hole up inside, Malú," Mom said.

"I can't?"

Mom walked over and hooked her arm through mine. I

had no choice but to let her pull me back down the unfamiliar hallway.

"Come on," she said. "You can finish working on that later."

"Can I bring my skateboard?"

"If it will get you out of this funk," Mom said with a sigh. "Just be careful."

"I will." She was always paranoid that I'd break a bone if I so much as looked at my skateboard. Or, maybe even worse, fall and show my underwear to the world.

In the hallway Mom fumbled with the key in the lock, when the door across the hall opened and a pair of dark shiny eyes peered out. A tiny old woman waved at us.

"Hola, muchachas, everything okay?" the woman asked.

She stepped out from behind her door wearing a white housedress with a unicorn print. Her hair was gathered into a stubby bunny tail at the nape of her neck. Little salt-and-pepper tendrils escaped and curled around her ears.

"Hola, señora," Mom said with a smile. "No problem, just the lock acting a little funny."

Mom finally managed to lock the door and pulled the key out with a frustrated yank.

"That lock is a pain in the nalgas," the woman said knowingly. She walked over to Mom and grabbed her hands like she'd known her forever. I could tell Mom was a little startled.

"Soy Oralia Bernal," she said. "Welcome to the building."

"Gracias, Señora Oralia," Mom said. "I'm Magaly Morales. This is my daughter, María Luisa."

Mom insisted on introducing me to people by my full name, which was so annoying.

"Hi," I said. Señora Oralia shuffled over to me, grabbed my hands in hers, and squeezed them. Her hands were brown, darker than mine, and covered in faint wrinkles that made them look like paper bags someone had balled up and then tried to smooth out. They reminded me of my abuela's hands. Except Abuela never wore nail polish, and Señora Oralia's nails were painted a glittery purple.

"Bueno, bienvenidos," Señora Oralia said.

She looked between us and smiled. I caught the glint of a silver tooth. It reminded me of a character in a book I'd read, and for a moment I wondered if Señora Oralia was a witch too.

"This is a good building. Quiet," Señora Oralia said. "If you need anything, just come by. I'm here all the time, except when I'm not."

She let out a raspy chuckle.

"That's so nice of you," Mom said. "We're going out to explore, but I'm sure we'll see you again soon."

"Sí, claro," Señora Oralia said with a little wave. "Have a good time, muchachas."

I forced a smile and watched as she slipped back into her apartment.

"She seems nice," Mom said once Señora Oralia was gone.

"I guess."

"So, there are a lot of great-looking places around here. I did a little research online. How about Ethiopian? They serve your meal on a round tray covered with a big piece of injera and everyone shares."

"What's injera?" I asked.

"It's like a spongy sourdough bread," Mom said. "You use it instead of utensils to eat your food. Neat, right?"

She grinned like it was the most exciting thing she'd ever heard. There was only one thing I really wanted to know.

"Is there cilantro in Ethiopian food?" I asked.

"Hmm, I'm not sure," Mom said. "But we'll check, okay?"

We headed down our street, me rolling slowly on my skateboard next to Mom.

"You nervous about school?"

"Nope," I said, and gave her a big, fake smile. "It's always been my dream to be the new kid in seventh grade."

"I'm so glad you got my dry sense of humor," Mom said. "It's okay to be nervous, you know."

"Punks don't get nervous," I said, even though I *was* nervous. Super nervous.

"That makes one of us," she said. "Maybe I should try being a punk."

I rolled my eyes, but Mom didn't even notice. Her brow furrowed the way it does when she's in a work trance, like she was already thinking about her great new job and had forgotten all about me.

"Your school is close if you want to do a walk-by," Mom

said. “Might be good to get the lay of the land.”

“I can wait.” I wanted to avoid going anywhere near that place until I absolutely had no choice.

“I think you’re going to like it here, Malú,” Mom said. “There’s so much art and culture and history; it’s right up your alley.”

“Have you noticed that even the sky looks different here?” I asked, changing the subject. “I think it’s less *blue*.”

I glanced up at the trees that lined our street.

“Please don’t take your eyes off the sidewalk when you’re riding that thing,” Mom warned.

“And there’s no Spanish moss,” I said. “No lovebugs, either.”

“I won’t miss having to wash those bugs off the car,” Mom said with a shudder. “To be honest, I won’t even miss having a car!”

“I’ll miss them,” I said, even though I’d never thought twice about the bugs when I was home.

“Malú, we’re in Chicago,” Mom said. “You’re acting like we’ve moved to another planet.”

“I feel like I’m on another planet,” I said, pushing my foot harder against the sidewalk to gather speed. “I’m just waiting for the flying monkeys to appear.”

Mom laughed as I passed by her on my skateboard.

Chapter 4

Mom spent the week dragging me around the city to explore. We rode on the "L," the trains that travel all over Chicago. We went to Lake Michigan, which was freezing cold for September and not salty like the Atlantic. We saw SUE the T. rex at the Field Museum, and Seurat's people in the park, painted from tiny dots, at the Art Institute. We visited the biggest public library building I'd ever seen, where I got a new library card and a stack of books. We had egg custard buns and tea at a bakery in Chinatown. And we almost got swept up into a White Sox game before Mom came to her senses and remembered she didn't even like baseball.

Then one day, while searching for a bookstore Mom wanted to visit, I saw Laurie's Planet of Sound. It looked even cooler than Dad had described it. I thought about asking Mom if we could check it out, but I didn't. It felt too weird to think about being in someone else's record store. Plus, I figured Mom wouldn't be interested. But it didn't matter because she spotted her bookstore before I could say anything.

By Sunday morning all I wished for, besides going back home, was to be left alone with my music, my zine supplies, and my denial that school was starting. SuperMexican, of course, was not having it.

"Let's go get some breakfast," Mom said. "I saw a cute little coffee shop on my way to the train the other day."

"No, thanks. I'm just going to eat some cereal."

"Come on," she said, yanking my comforter. "It's our last day before school starts. Let's have a nice breakfast together just like old times, okay?"

I pulled the blanket back over myself.

"I'll bring some work," Mom offered. "You won't even have to talk to me."

"You promise?"

"Just kidding," Mom said. "Let's go."

Grrrr.

"And can you please put on a clean shirt? You've been wearing the same one for days now."

I sniffed my T-shirt. "Smells fine to me."

The coffee shop we walked to had a bright red awning that said CALACA COFFEE. The large glass window was decorated with colorful skulls, marigolds, and dancing skeletons. I had to admit, Mom was right. It did look kind of cool.

Inside we were greeted by a life-sized papier-mâché skeleton that looked like Frida Kahlo with her blackbird eyebrows. A skeleton monkey was perched in her bony arms. It was Frida's pet monkey, Fulang-Chang. Frida was one of my favorite artists and not just because I was almost named after her. I like that she painted about herself and her life and that she was outspoken. She was pretty punk rock! Near Frida was a shelf crammed full of books. I liked this place already.

There were steps leading up to a loft area with floor seating where pillows of mismatched colors, patterns, and sizes surrounded a few short tables. A woman with a bright pink stripe running through her dark hair cleared off a table. The sleeves of her shirtdress were rolled up to her elbows, revealing colorful tattoos on both arms. I couldn't stop staring.

"Can we sit up there, Mom?"

I set one foot on the first step leading to the loft. Mom looked like she was going to say no, but the tattooed woman noticed us before she could.

"You can sit anywhere," the woman said. "I'll bring you some menus in a minute, okay?"

Mom smiled in acknowledgment and headed up to the loft.

"I'm going to look around," I said.

"Go for it." Mom pulled her planner out of her bag.

I slid my skateboard under our table and wandered toward the ordering area.

The display case beneath the counter was filled with

pan dulce, sweet Mexican breads, that I remembered eating when I visited my abuelos. Each tray had a little sign in Spanish and English indicating the names of the different types of bread: LA CONCHA/THE SHELL; EL BIGOTE/THE MUSTACHE; LA OREJA/THE EAR; EL MARRANITO/THE PIG. They were named after what they looked like. My favorite was always the concha because it had sections of sweet, colorful icing on top that I liked to peel off and eat separately.

The walls behind the counter were covered with wooden animal masks and bright tin suns, moons, and skeletons. So many skeletons.

Then I saw something super familiar: cardboard record sleeves decorating a different wall. I got excited because there were some punky eighties-looking bands. Mixed in with them were fifties rock-and-roll singers with greased pompadours, and Mexican singers with big mustaches and bigger hats. I moved closer to get a better look at the album covers. I recognized a few of them as people Mom listened to sometimes.

When I walked back to our table, Mom was talking to the woman who had greeted us.

"Ana, this is my daughter, María Luisa," Mom said.

I plopped down on a big, velvety orange-and-red pillow.

"Malú," I said. "Hi."

I tried not to stare at her pink hair and tattoos. She looked like she might be Mexican, but I had never seen another Mexican punk.

"Mrs. Hidalgo owns the coffee shop," Mom said. "And

guess what. She's Señora Oralia's daughter. You know, from our building?"

"What a small world, right? I grew up in that building," Mrs. Hidalgo said. "Your mother tells me you're at JGP Middle School."

I gave her a puzzled look.

"That's what we call it sometimes, JGP, for José Guadalupe Posada, or just Posada."

"Oh," I said. "I see."

"My son is going into the seventh grade too," she went on. "He's not here today, but you should meet him. Ask around for José Hidalgo, okay? He's hard to miss."

She winked at me and pulled an order pad out of her apron pocket. I nodded even though I could not see myself asking around for someone I didn't know.

"Now let me get your order so you ladies can eat already. I hope you're okay with vegetarian food."

"Vegetarian is great," I said.

"I highly recommend the Soyrizo breakfast tacos," Mrs. Hidalgo said. "We make our own."

"Is there cilantro in it?" I asked suspiciously.

"No cilantro," Mrs. Hidalgo said. "We can sprinkle some on top if you'd like."

Mom laughed. "I think she'll pass."

"Got it," Mrs. Hidalgo said with a nod. I felt myself blushing, hoping Mrs. Hidalgo didn't think it was weird that I didn't want cilantro.

"And a coffee, please," I said.

"I'll have coffee too," Mom said, closing her menu. "And the yogurt and granola, thanks."

Mrs. Hidalgo jotted down our order then tucked her pencil into her apron pocket.

"Don't hesitate to let me know if you need anything, Magaly," she said.

Mom smiled and thanked her. Once Mrs. Hidalgo was out of earshot, Mom shook her head.

"Vegetarian Mexicans," she said. "I'll never understand that."

"Don't be so closed-minded, Mom," I said.

"Point taken." Mom sipped her water. "This is great, right? We've met some nice people. Maybe even a new school friend?"

I slumped back against the wall and picked at my black nail polish.

"You should find José at school," Mom said. "It'll be good for you to have someone to hang out with."

"Thanks for the concern," I said. "And do you think you could stop introducing me as María Luisa?"

"That's your name, isn't it?"

"You know what I mean, Mom," I said. "It's bad enough I have to be here at all without people calling me María Luisa, too."

"Malú, I can't imagine it feels good to be angry or annoyed about everything all the time," Mom said.

"How would you feel if you were me? If you were moved a thousand miles away from home? Against your will."

"Chicago isn't a thousand miles away from Gainesville," Mom replied.

"You're right. I looked it up," I said. "It's one thousand and fifty miles away. That's practically at the end of the Earth."

"Ay, Malú, you're so dramatic."

A young guy stopped at our table and placed a mug in front of each of us. I brought the steaming coffee to my face and took a careful sip. It tasted earthy and sweet, like cinnamon and piloncillo. The last time I visited my abuela, she had a big cone of piloncillo that we'd chip off into our coffee to sweeten it.

"Seriously," I said. "If I were a sailor back in Columbus's day, I'd be afraid we were going to drop off into an abyss and be eaten by a giant sea serpent."

"For your information, Columbus knew the world was round," Mom said. "He just thought it was smaller than it is."

I shot Mom the iciest look I could give. She had a habit of turning everything into a learning opportunity.

Our food arrived, and I inspected my Soyrizo for signs of cilantro, my culinary archnemesis, just in case.

"All clear?" Mom asked.

I nodded and took a bite.

"It's a big deal to be offered this visiting professor fellowship," Mom said. "And it's not forever, so let's make the best of our time here."

"You make it sound like that's really easy," I said.

Mom closed her eyes and took a deep breath before opening them again.

"I can assure you that being a grump about it is only going to make things harder," she said. "Give it a chance, Malú. You might actually like Chicago."

"What's to like about moving to a strange place?" I said. "I don't know anyone here."

"You'll make friends and do things here just like you would back home."

Of course. Wasn't that what adults were supposed to say?

"You'll figure it out," Mom said. "I hope you'll at least try, for your own sake and for my sanity. No more sulking, okay?" She gave my braid a little tug.

Sometimes I wondered if Mom even remembered what it's like to be a kid.

"How is that soy chorizo?"

"It's *Soyrizo,*" I said. "Animal-free and delicious."

Mom closed her eyes and took another a deep breath, but this time a small smile crept onto her lips.

✂✂✂

That night I tried not to think about school starting the next day. It wasn't easy, especially when my phone buzzed with a text from Dad wishing me luck. I decided to distract myself by doodling.

I dug the little yellow box of worry dolls out of my bag and dumped them onto the desktop. *Worrying about stuff is so not punk, Malú.* But I grabbed a sheet of paper and wrote down my worries anyway.

When I was done, I gathered the worry dolls and crawled under the ugly flower print comforter. I didn't really believe that six tiny stick figures had magical powers that could take away my worries. Still, I lifted my pillow and lined them up in a row underneath. I turned off the light and climbed into bed. Then I buried my face into the pillow so that Mom wouldn't hear me crying.

Going to a new school where I won't know any-one or where anything is.

What if I never like Chicago?

Not seeing Dad. Would he eventually forget about me?

WORRIED? ME?

Mom not letting me be myself. But what else is new?

What if no one at school likes the same music I like? What if I never find my people?

Never going home again. What if Mom decides to stay forever?

Chapter 5

When my alarm went off the next morning, I hid under the comforter. My eyes felt dry from crying. They stung like when I'd been at the beach all day and gotten too much salt water in them.

Mom knocked on the door and poked her head in.

"We may not have much in the fridge, but we have coffee," she said, triumphantly holding up a package of beans from Calaca. "You want?"

"I need," I said, peeking out at her.

"I'll do some grocery shopping today," Mom said. "We can pick up something to eat on the way to school."

"Can I walk to school alone?"

"Walk alone? No way," Mom said.

"Please," I said. "It's not like I'll get lost."

"I know, but it's your first day. I want to see you off."

"Fine, whatever." I kicked the heavy comforter to the floor.

"Great, I'm excited too," Mom said. "Coffee in ten minutes."

I rolled my eyes and dragged myself out of bed.

I unpacked a bag until I found my green jeans. I put on my favorite Blondie T-shirt and my silver-sequined Chuck Taylors.

Dad gave me the sneakers last year after I read *The Wonderful Wizard of Oz*. In the movie version Dorothy wears ruby slippers, but in the book she wears silver shoes that she takes off the Wicked Witch of the East when the house lands on her and kills her. It's not until the end of the story that Dorothy learns she can wish on the shoes to take her back home to Kansas. I'd been wearing them for a week now, but they seemed to have lost their magic, because no matter how many times I closed my eyes and clicked my heels, I was still in Chicago. Never back home.

A hole had grown on the sole of one shoe where the rubber had worn away. *Nothing a little duct tape can't fix*. I found my roll and did a quick patch job, stretching a strip of tape across the bottom of my shoe and over the sides.

In the bathroom, I looked at my reflection in the mirror and made a face when I remembered one of Dad's favorite jokes.

"You got your Mexican from Mom and your punk from me," he'd say.

I had the Mexican going on for sure: brown skin and thick brown hair that was lighter than Mom's but darker than Dad's and that I usually wore in two braids. I had

Mom's dark eyes too. My punk, on the other hand, was terribly lacking.

I washed my face and braided my hair like I did every morning. Before I left the bathroom, I noticed Mom's makeup bag on the counter and got an idea. I dug around until I found a black eyeliner pencil. I opened the cap and squinted closely at the tip, unsure where to start, then set it gently against the inside corner of my eye and drew up, tracing my eyelid to the top. I imagined that I was coloring inside the lines of a coloring book, but the pencil was waxy and smudgy and an eye is nothing like a flat sheet of paper.

My hand trembled as I moved the pencil closer. I did my best not to poke myself. There's nothing punk about an eye injury. Unless it happened in a mosh pit, of course.

As I drew what I hoped looked like wing tips, I thought about the singer with the dark, dramatic eyes on the album cover at Spins & Needles. That was the look I was going for. I found the glittery black eye shadow Mom had used last Halloween and swiped some over each eyelid. I filled my lips with the darkest lipstick I could find to finish the look.

In the end, the cat eyes were crooked and my eyelids felt sticky and heavy, but I definitely looked a little more punk.

"Coffee's poured," Mom called from the kitchen.

"Coming," I said, stuffing everything back into her makeup bag.

I headed to the kitchen, where Mom leaned against the counter, writing out a grocery list. As I grabbed the mug of coffee Mom had placed on the table for me, I noticed my fingers were covered in glitter and eyeliner. I wiped them across my jeans.

"Ready?" she asked.

She looked up, pen in hand, and stared at my face for a few seconds.

"Ohhh no," she said, shaking her head. "I don't think so."

"What is it, Mom?" I asked, like there was absolutely nothing out of the ordinary.

"What it is, is that you are not going to school looking like *that*."

"What's wrong with how I look?"

Mom gave me a get-serious stare. "Do you really need a rundown?" she asked. "You're twelve years old, for starters."

"Almost thirteen," I said.

"Semantics. You're twelve, señorita."

"Please, Mom," I said. "Pleeease."

"It's your first day at a new school," she said. "Is this really the impression you want to make on people who don't know anything about you?"

"It's just makeup."

"If you're interested in wearing makeup, I can teach you how to apply it properly," Mom said. "Like una señorita."

I thought about the singer on the album cover and wondered who taught her how to apply makeup.

"I think it looks cool," I said. "I was going for a different look."

"Well, in that case, you succeeded. You look like Nosferatu."

"Who's Nosferatu?"

"A creepy vampire," Mom said. "Look him up."

"You're so mean," I said.

Mom's eyes trailed down to my torn jeans and beat-up, duct-taped sneakers.

"When I was your age, I couldn't even afford to buy new clothes," she said. "I just don't get it. You look like una huerfanita."

"A what?" I asked.

"Una huerfanita," Mom repeated. "An orphan."

"I do not look like an orphan," I said, picturing Oliver Twist asking for more porridge.

Mom attempted to stick a finger through a hole on the side of my jeans.

I jumped out of her reach. "Mom!"

She stared at me with a frown on her face.

"Please?" I said. "Can I just do this one thing?"

"You'll never ask for anything else again, right?"

"Exactly," I said.

Mom stared at me for a few more uncomfortably long seconds.

"I can't imagine they allow seventh graders to come to school made up like that," she said. "And it's going to take forever to wash that off."

I could see in Mom's face that she wasn't happy about it, but I couldn't help smiling.

"Is that a yes?" I asked.

"This isn't a yes," Mom said. "This is a go-ahead-and-learn-the-hard-way, Malú."

"Yes!" I whooped.

"If I get a call from school about it being distracting, this nonsense is over," she said, wagging a finger. "You hear me?"

"Why would this be distracting?" I asked, batting my sticky eyelashes.

Mom sighed and stuffed her list into her purse.

I couldn't believe she had actually agreed to let me go to school wearing makeup.

"Vámonos, creature of the night," she said, shaking her head.

Chapter 6

Finding homeroom was easy. Walking into it was a little harder. I stalled a bit, looking at my schedule and then at the number next to the door. It was definitely the right room, and I knew I couldn't avoid it forever. As soon as I stepped through the doorway, it felt like all eyes turned to me.

"It's a little early for Halloween," someone called out.

A few kids sitting in the back of the room burst into laughter.

Ms. Hernandez, the homeroom teacher according to my schedule, stared at me for a few seconds too long before waving me in.

"Yes," she said, searching her desktop for something. "I may need to talk to you, but go ahead and sit for now while I get through roll call."

My stomach twisted like a pretzel. Why would she need to talk to me? *Please don't let it be about my makeup.* I scanned the room and hurried to the first empty seat I saw. I'd barely slinked down into my chair when the girl sitting across the aisle spoke to me.

"You're new, right?" she asked, chewing on the candy necklace she wore.

"Um, yeah," I said.

"What's up with your makeup?"

I got the same feeling inside as when Mom would start in on me about my clothes. Like I had to get ready for battle. I knew the girl wasn't just curious; she was judging me.

"What's up with yours?" I asked. The words spilled out before I realized it was not only rude but a pointless retort, since she didn't appear to wear anything but lip gloss.

"María Luisa O'Neill-Morales?" Ms. Hernandez called, looking around the room.

I cringed at the sound of my name and raised my hand.

"Ms. Hernandez," I said. "You can call me Malú."

She nodded and marked something on her attendance sheet.

"What kind of name is that anyway?" the girl asked. "It's weird."

She said it loud enough for the kids around us to hear. She said it like there was something wrong with my name. Like there was something wrong with me.

"Don't you mean *unusual*?" the girl in front of her said, and giggled. She wore a candy necklace too.

"Sorry, yeah, that's what I meant," she said. "What are you? You're not Mexican, right?"

What are you? I was used to getting some version of that question, especially when people heard my name. I wasn't always sure how to answer. Sometimes it just seemed easier to blurt out what Mom calls my pie chart: half Mexican, half fill-in-the-blank with the names of a bunch of different European countries. I didn't think this girl would care much about my pie chart.

She looked at me, waiting, daring me to say something. I had the feeling that no matter what I said, she wasn't going to like it.

"I'm half Mexican," I said.

"Half Mexican, huh? Psssh." It sounded like gas escaping from a bottle of soda.

She looked at me from head to toe then turned back to her friend, swinging her long curls in the process. She and her friend could have been twins. They both had dark glossy hair that hung down their backs, and their bangs were straightened and hair sprayed.

I pulled my notebook out of my bag and wrote down some ideas for a new zine. I tried to imagine that I was in a bubble that could protect me from this new place and this girl. Like the one Glinda the Good Witch travels inside.

"Selena Ramirez," Ms. Hernandez called out.

The girl who had been talking to me raised her hand without turning away from her friend. They huddled together and giggled. I knew what they were laughing about because every so often the other girl, the one who answered to Diana during roll call, looked over and made eye contact.

"Malú, could you please come here?" Ms. Hernandez asked. My bubble burst.

I slid out of my chair and heard Selena and Diana whisper *ooooohhh* as I passed by.

When I walked up to Ms. Hernandez's desk, she was flipping through a thin, spiral-bound book. Printed on the cover was *José Guadalupe Posada M. S. Student Code of Conduct.*

"I could be wrong, Malú, but according to this, I think your makeup is a dress-code violation," she said, putting the manual down. "You'll need to go to the auditorium."

"Am I in trouble?" I asked. Punks don't worry about getting in trouble. But this punk still had to answer to her mom.

"No, of course not. It's only the first day of school," Ms. Hernandez said. "But Principal Rivera wants everyone to be clear on the dress code." She held out a copy of the manual for me to take.

"Collect your things and head down there," she said. "It's at the end of hall."

I nodded and walked back to my desk. I could feel Selena watching me as I stuffed my notebook and the code of conduct booklet into my backpack.

"Welcome to Posada, María Luisa," she whispered before she and Diana broke into a fit of giggles.

the STORY OF A NAME

(my name!)

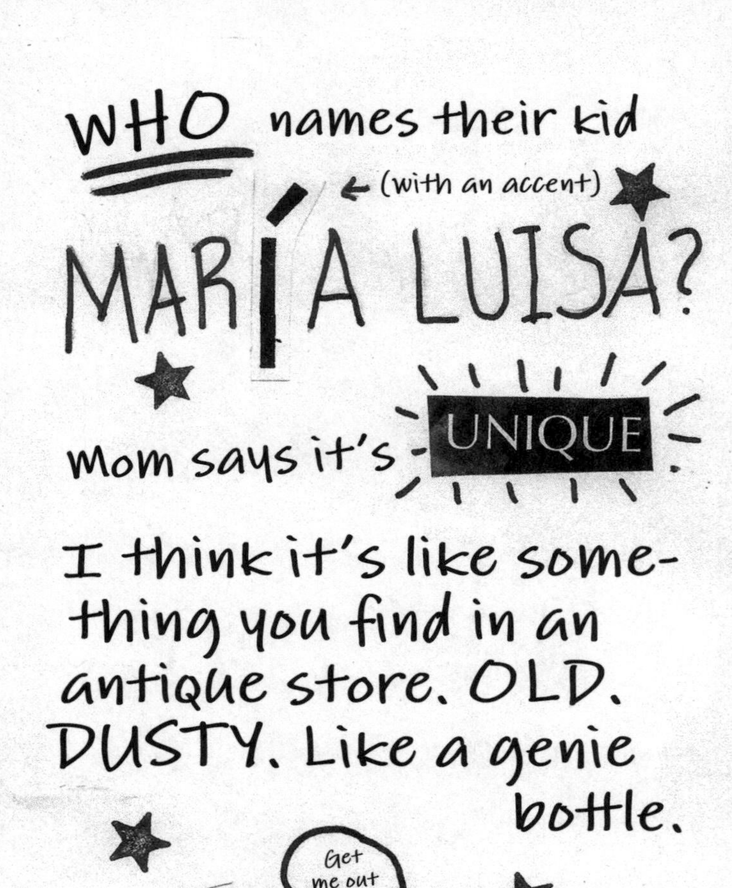

WHO names their kid (with an accent) MARÍA LUISA?

Mom says it's UNIQUE

I think it's like something you find in an antique store. OLD. DUSTY. Like a genie bottle.

Except it doesn't grant wishes.

Self-portrait with cool T-shirt.

Dad wanted a name that was Punky.

Mom wanted something Traditional.

They couldn't agree.

(surprise.)

Then one night they watched a movie about a famous painter & agreed.

But a few days later while reading a book about Frida Kahlo, Mom came across . . .

María Luisa

AKA
María Luisa Block
AKA

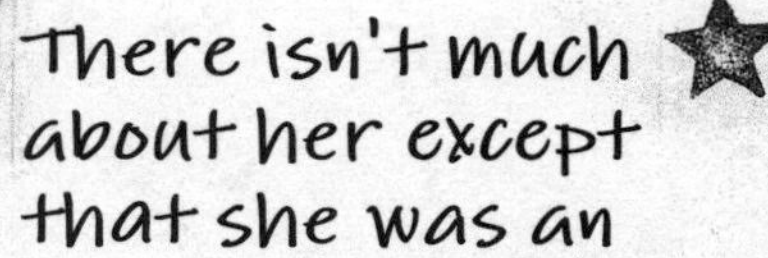

There isn't much about her except that she was an artist too, but she is in a photo with Frida and her husband Diego Rivera. Malú is barely in the frame.

Like she wasn't the focus of the picture. Mom says Frida is so famous there are probably plenty of "Fridas" in the world and who wants to be one more "Frida" anyway?

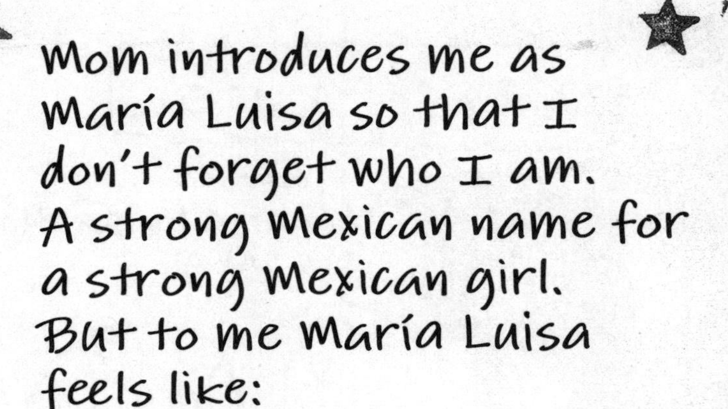

Mom introduces me as María Luisa so that I don't forget who I am. A strong Mexican name for a strong Mexican girl. But to me María Luisa feels like:

"NORMAL?"

But I feel like this:

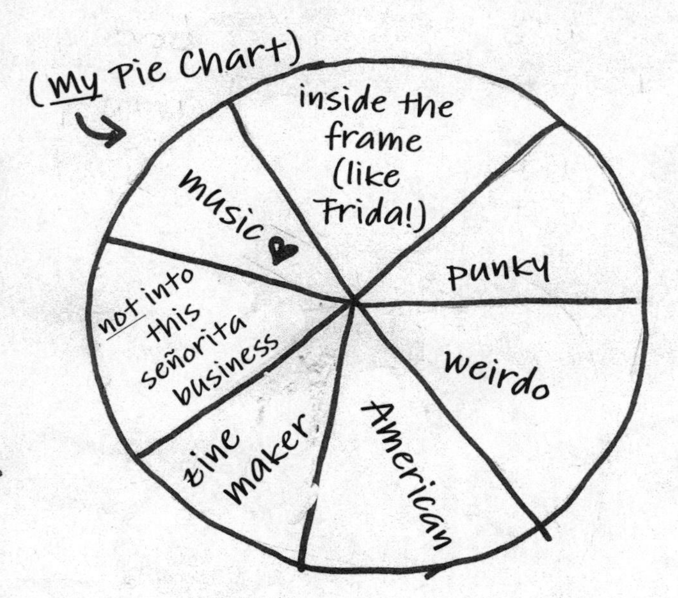

It's like Mom's María Luisa and my Malú are two different people.

GOOD BYE
M

Chapter 7

"Everyone, please sit toward the front," a man called from the stage. He was short and skinny with glasses and a beard that matched the little bit of hair on either side of his head. He waved his hands wildly, urging us forward.

I looked around at the other kids who'd been sent by their homeroom teachers and tried to figure out why. One kid had on a T-shirt with a cartoon character mooning everyone. Another kid had pants belted just above his knees. Some kids were harder to guess, but we were a herd of dress-code violators, and the man on the stage was corralling us.

A boy with blue hair sat down in the seat in front of me. His hair looked punk, but nothing else about him did. He reminded me of someone out of a Beverly Cleary book, with his plaid short-sleeve button-down shirt, cuffed jeans, and black Converse high-tops. Like a brown-skinned, blue-haired Henry Huggins.

The man came down from the stage and handed out copies of the student code of conduct.

"I'm Mr. Jackson, a guidance counselor here at Posada," he said. "And *you* are the lucky few who got picked for a personal introduction to the school's dress code. I need everyone to take a few minutes to read over the list on page two."

I opened the copy Ms. Hernandez had given me and read. No leggings as pants. No pajama bottoms. No clothes with inappropriate graphics or language. No spaghetti straps or crop tops. No flip-flops or slippers. No physical alterations that are deemed potentially disruptive, including, but not limited to, unnatural hair color, makeup, or piercings. No pants hanging below the waist. Skirts and shorts must pass the "fingertip test." The list seemed to go on.

Mr. Jackson passed out another sheet of paper.

"This is a letter to your parent or guardian," he said. "Please fill in your dress-code violation. These need to be signed and returned to your homeroom teachers tomorrow."

"This is ridiculous," someone muttered.

"And unfair," the boy with the blue hair added. "You know how long it took me to get my hair this color? All summer, Mr. Jackson. Mexican hair ain't easy to dye."

Everyone laughed.

"How is my tank top the same as old raccoon eyes over here?" a girl asked, gesturing at me.

The blue-haired boy turned around and we made eye contact.

"Radical, dude," he said in jokey surfer speech before turning back. "Mr. Jackson, my hair is me showing school spirit. I thought that would be appreciated."

Mr. Jackson smiled. "I can see that," he said. "But these are the rules, guys. Don't like them? Figure out a constructive way to express yourselves."

I imagined Mom's I-told-you-so look as I filled in my dress-code violation: disruptive physical alteration. In parentheses, I wrote *rad makeup*.

Mr. Jackson spent the rest of our time in the auditorium trying to figure out ways each of us could fix our dress-code violations for the day. The kid with the cartoon character on his shirt was sent to the restroom to turn the shirt inside out. The girl with the tank top was given a POSADA PHYS. ED. DEPARTMENT T-shirt to put on. The boy with the blue hair was told to come back "with a normal hair color" the next day.

"What's 'normal,' right?" the boy asked me as he stuffed the letter into the back pocket of his jeans and headed to class. One by one we were dismissed.

"Wow," Mr. Jackson said, stopping in front of me. "What's going on with this look?"

"It's punk," I said with a shrug.

"Well," Mr. Jackson said. "You're going to have to do punk some other way, young lady. Go ask the school nurse for a wash cloth, see how much of that you can scrub off."

He handed me a hall pass and moved on to the next kid. I left in search of the nurse's office, feeling not at all punk.

Chapter 8

At lunch I grabbed an orange plastic tray and stared at the chafing dishes full of food, unsure what to take.

"Yummy, right?" A tall, long-haired kid in front of me grinned as a lunch lady dropped a spoonful of something yellow that looked like creamed corn onto his tray.

I looked back at the food on the other side of the plastic divider.

"I can't even decide. It all looks so good," I said.

"I have a system," he said. "I choose my food blobs by color. No neutrals. Only brights."

"Does that work?"

"Not really," he said. "It's all terrible." He picked up the instrument case he'd set on the floor and moved on down the line.

"Awesome," I said. But I took his advice. I avoided the gross meaty brown blobs and settled on a green blob, an orange blob, and a red blob.

The cafeteria was noisy with kids laughing and talking sometimes in English, sometimes in Spanish, and sometimes in a combination bouncing back and forth between languages. It was strange to hear so much Spanish. Back home I almost never heard it unless Mom spoke it or happened to be listening to something in Spanish.

I found a place to sit alone near the entrance for an easy escape, should I need it. It's a known fact that behind a book is always a good place for hiding and people-watching, so I pulled out my copy of *The Outsiders,* the book assigned to us in English class. From my hiding place I looked around for where I might fit in. Where were my people?

I watched the kid from the lunch line sit down at a table with other kids who had instrument cases. The blue-haired boy who had been in the auditorium that morning slipped into a seat at another table.

Nearby, Selena sat with Diana and a larger group. I watched them like I was an anthropologist. Being an anthropologist was my second career choice after musician in a punk band, so I studied Selena and her friends as if they were a newly discovered culture.

The boys wore baggy jeans, puffy basketball sneakers, and huge shirts. The girls all wore similar outfits of tight jeans and T-shirts with stuff like CUTIE and SRSLY printed on them. Like Selena, they all wore candy necklaces.

There should be something about candy accessories and misspelled words on clothes in the dress code.

Selena looked in my direction, and I slid down in my seat a little, hoping she hadn't spotted me. Unfortunately, she had. She got up and walked toward me, arriving in a cloud of vanilla-scented perfume. She stood there as if waiting for an invitation to sit, but I didn't take my eyes off my book even though nothing was coming into focus. Selena wasn't leaving.

"Hey, María Luisa," she finally said, sitting down next to me.

"It's Malú," I said.

"So did you get in trouble this morning?"

"No," I said. "Are you disappointed?"

She stuck her thumb under the elastic of her candy necklace, pulling on a pink candy circle. She brought it to her mouth and bit into it. The circle cracked, and a tiny piece of pink flew onto my tray.

"Look, I'm not here to bother you," she said, giving me a sly smile that said otherwise.

Dad said being punk was about being open-minded, and that included giving people the benefit of the doubt, but I wasn't convinced Selena was trying to be nice.

"Where'd you move from?" she asked.

"Florida."

"Florida, huh? You ever go to Disney?"

I shook my head.

"I've been twice," she said. "With my dance school."

This was probably when having friends came in handy.

I was like a nation of one in the cafeteria with no one to help defend the territory.

"I know it's probably hard being new, so I thought you could use some help," Selena went on, finally getting to the point of her visit.

"What kind of help?" I asked, taking the bait.

"You know, someone to teach you how things are around here," she said. "Trust me, it's a good thing they made you wash off that makeup. Only a coconut would do that kind of thing."

"What's a coconut?" I asked.

"Of course you don't know what that is," Selena said. "Never mind."

She looked at the hole in my jeans and made a face.

"The point is, try not to be a weirdo. If you can."

She said the word *weirdo* like it was a terrible disease I didn't want to catch. I started to feel my ears burn like they do when I'm angry.

"I just want to read my book, okay?" I said, hoping she'd lose interest and move on soon.

"You see those guys over there?" she asked, not taking the hint. "Why do you think they're sitting alone?"

She pointed to where the blue-haired boy sat with another kid. They didn't look alone to me.

"Weirdos," she whispered. "You don't want to end up at that table."

I glanced at the table where her friends sat looking our way.

"I think I'd rather be at that table than yours," I said.

"Is that how you treat someone who's trying to be a friend?" Selena pretended to look hurt. "Listen, I know a weirdo when I see one," she said. "And I'm trying to save you from yourself, María Luisa."

"Can you just go back to your table and leave me alone?"

"Fine," Selena said, getting up. "Let me know if you change your mind." She looked down at my shoes. "Is that tape?"

I stared at the duct tape that peeked out over the sides of my shoes.

"Wow," she said. "You really do need help."

She made a disgusted face and walked off, leaving me feeling like something really low. Like a piece of tape stuck to the bottom of someone's shoe.

Chapter 9

As soon as I opened the front door after school, I wished for a secret entrance that would let me go straight to my room without having to face Mom.

"I'm in the kitchen," she called out. "Come, I want to hear all about your day."

I dragged my feet to the kitchen, where Mom was almost finished painting one wall a bright tangerine color. She was wearing her work-around-the-house clothes: overalls and an old MEChA T-shirt.

"You like it? I'm not going to paint the entire place, but I thought it could use a little color."

"It's nice," I said, thinking no amount of paint would make me like this place.

"Speaking of color," she said. "What happened to your makeup?"

She asked it in a way that sounded like she'd already figured it out but wanted to hear me say it.

"Yeah, about that . . ." I said, digging into my backpack. "Here."

Mom took the sheet; a frown appeared on her face as she read it.

"What did I tell you? First day and you have a strike against you."

"It's not a strike, Mom," I said. "It's a warning. Anyway, at least my underwear wasn't showing like another kid who got called into the auditorium."

"Pen," Mom said, and held out her hand. "Let's try for less punk rocker and more señorita from now on."

"Can't I be both?" I asked.

She gave me her I'm-not-joking look and handed me the signed paper.

"Don't make me go through your clothes and throw out all those holey pants and shoes," she threatened.

"Fine," I said. "I'm going to call Dad. I promised I'd call as soon as I got home."

"Wait, did you make any friends?" she asked. She looked so hopeful. Sometimes I wonder if Mom even knows me.

"Not really."

"Not really, no? Or not really, yes, but you don't want to tell me?"

"Not really, not really," I said.

"How about José? Did you find out who he is?"

"I was too busy just trying to survive, Mom."

"Okay, don't tell me anything," Mom said, turning back to her painting. But I knew she wouldn't give up that easily.

I opened the refrigerator and grabbed a cheese stick.

"I was reading a little bit about your school's namesake today," Mom said. "Did you learn anything about José Guadalupe Posada yet?"

"Only that he was a pretty sharp dresser," I said. "I'm also guessing he was a very serious man."

"What in the world are you talking about?"

"There's a portrait of him in the hallway near the office," I said, and bit into my cheese stick.

"Cute," Mom said. "You might actually be interested in him. He was known for his political cartoons."

"Cartoons? Cool."

"And his calaveras," Mom went on.

"What's a calavera?" I asked.

"They're skulls, or skeletons," she explained. "Like the ones that are up at Calaca. Which, by the way, means—"

"Wow, Mom, how did you know?" I asked.

"What? About Posada?"

"No," I said. "That what I really needed after a long day at school was another history lesson."

"You are such a smart aleck," Mom said. "Anyway, he's an important figure in Mexican history. It's important to know about our history, Malú."

"*Your* history," I said. "I'm only half Mexican."

The conversation made me think of Selena. Another thing I didn't want to do after a long day at school.

"Our history," Mom repeated.

"Okay, SuperMexican."

I pictured Mom flying through the air with a rebozo cape billowing behind her and stifled a giggle.

"What's so funny?"

"Nothing," I said, but I had just gotten an idea for a zine.

"I'll make some pasta for dinner as soon as I finish this," Mom said. "Unless you want to help?"

"Sorry, gotta call Dad," I said. "Plus tons of homework."

"On the first day? Very strange."

"You wouldn't believe it," I said, backing away.

"Tell your dad I said hello."

I slipped out of the kitchen before Mom could stick a paintbrush in my hand.

In my room I threw myself on the bed and called Dad. The worry dolls were scattered everywhere, so I collected them and lined them up again neatly under my pillow. As I told Dad about being sent to the auditorium and about Selena making me feel like a freak, my insides clenched. It felt weird to say her name out loud to Dad. Like I was opening a door and letting Selena into my world, and I didn't want that at all.

After I hung up, I grabbed Dad's Walkman and hit play

on his mix. As the bouncy, poppy-punk song filled my head, my insides relaxed and expanded. I couldn't deal with the even-numbered problems that awaited me on pages nine and ten of my algebra book, so I pulled out my zine supplies instead.

SuperMexican

My mom, the superhero! (kind of . . .)

We all know that most moms have superpowers, right? Like the ability to figure out who ate the last of the chips and left the empty bag in the cabinet? (Wasn't me!) Or the power to know that you had a hard time getting out of bed because you were playing games on your phone way past your bedtime.

My mom has those powers and MORE! Because she isn't just any mom. She's . . .

SuperMexican!

SUPERMEXICAN is easy to spot. Unlike Clark Kent, she doesn't hide her real identity.

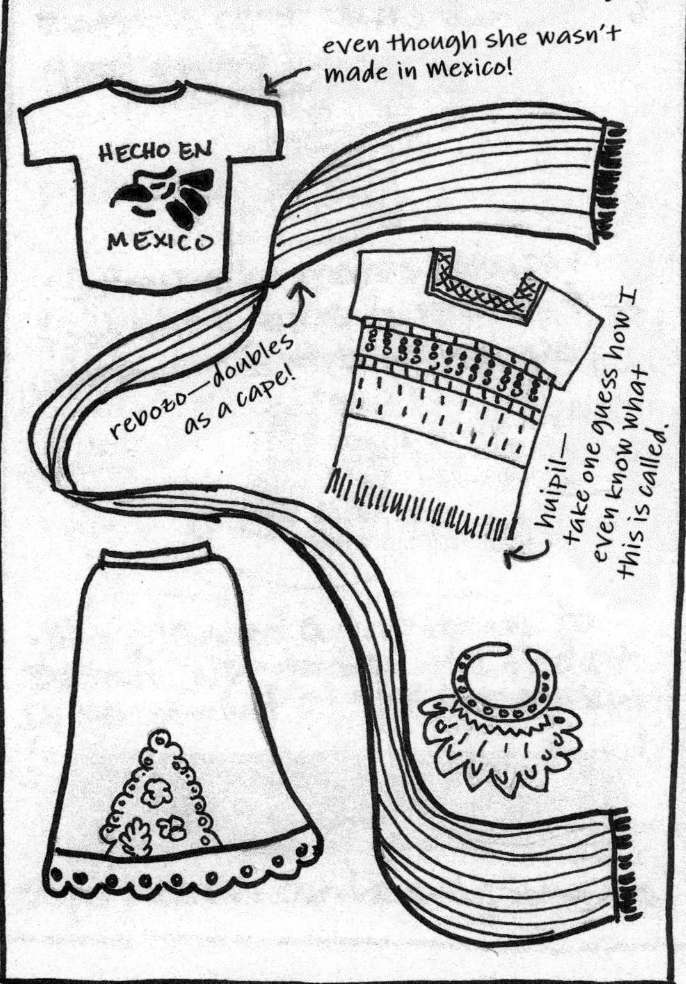

She absorbs everything she can about Mexico and about Mexicans in the United States. She's like an encyclopedia.

What's annoying is that she expects me to be like her and care too.

But her superpowers aren't ALL annoying. For example:

- She knows about a lot of authors and can recommend good books!

- When she makes Mexican food, she knows to make it without cilantro or hot peppers!

- She planned a trip to Detroit just so we could see the Frida and Diego exhibit at the art museum!

SuperMexican can be okay sometimes.

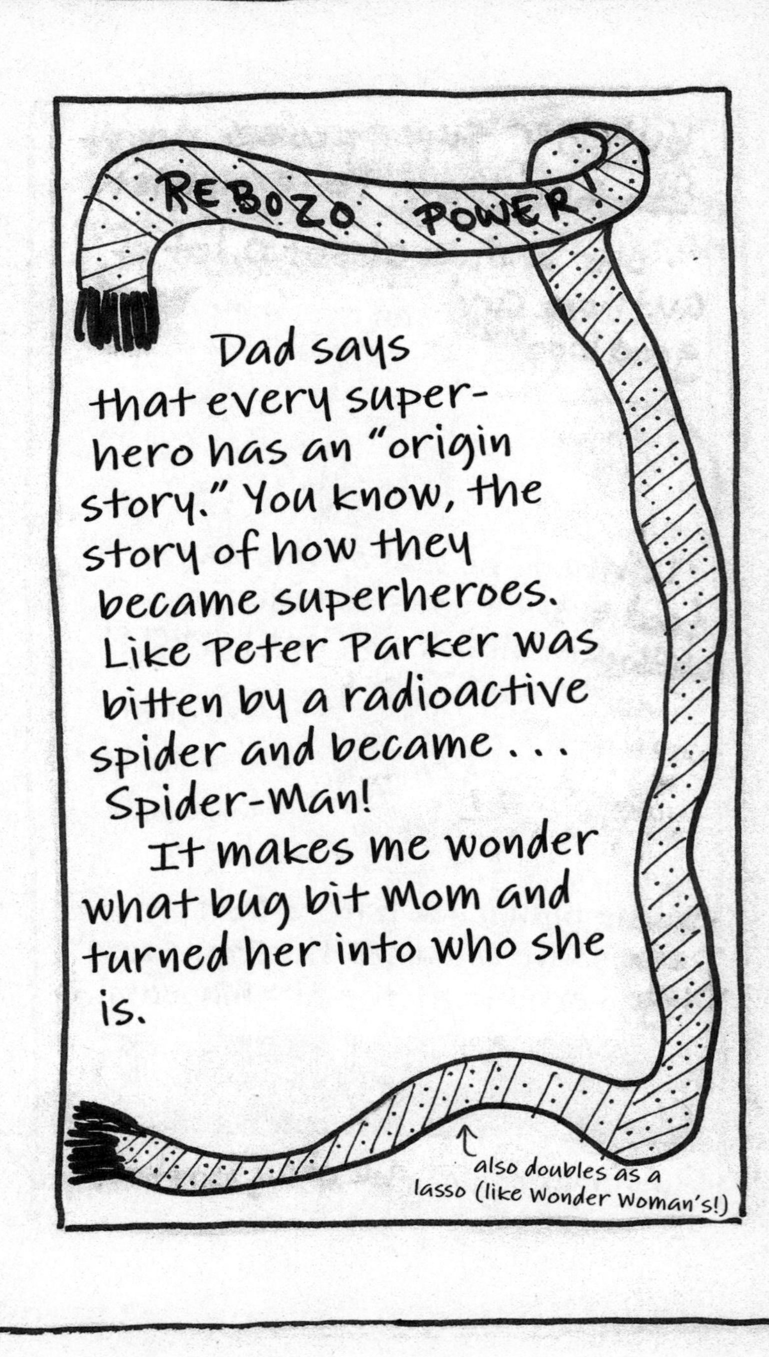
REBOZO POWER!
Dad says that every superhero has an "origin story." You know, the story of how they became superheroes. Like Peter Parker was bitten by a radioactive spider and became . . . Spider-Man!
It makes me wonder what bug bit Mom and turned her into who she is.
also doubles as a lasso (like Wonder Woman's!)

The thing I don't understand is why Mom cares so much. She isn't even Mexican! Abuela and Abuelo <u>are</u>, but Mom was born in

California used to be part of Mexico, though.

Does that count?

Sometimes I feel like Mom doesn't understand me. But I guess I don't really understand her either.

the End!

or is it?

Chapter 10

I made it my mission to avoid Selena as much as possible in the cafeteria, but it was like the fates conspired to bring us together in the worst possible place: Spanish class. There was one class for nonnative speakers, and all the rest of the periods were for fluent speakers. I was surprised to find out that I'd tested into the fluent class, since my Spanish sounded like it had been put in a blender and pulsed into a mess of sounds and letters. Selena's Spanish was, of course, perfecto.

"En español, señorita," Señor Ascencio reminded a girl named Beatriz who had asked to go to the bathroom. She let out a dramatic sigh.

"¿Puedo ir al baño, por favor?" she asked.

"Sí," he said. "Vaya rápidamente."

When class started, Señor Ascencio explained that we

each would have to create a family tree and write a short essay to go with it for our first big assignment due on Monday.

"¿Para cuándo, Señorita O'Neill-Morales?" he asked me, trying to confirm the due date for the assignment.

I sat up in my seat to answer, but before I could say anything, Selena interrupted.

"Señor Ascencio, María Luisa no habla español."

Some kids laughed, and I could feel my ears burn. Señor Ascencio ignored Selena and asked the question again.

"Para el lunes," I said through what felt like a mouthful of marbles.

"¡Muy bien, Señorita O'Neill-Morales!" Señor Ascencio read each word out loud as he wrote *para el lunes* on the board. "Para cuando vengan sus padres."

Great, the trees were going to be up at back-to-school night for everyone to see. Including Selena and her judgy little eyes.

I focused on finishing the workbook pages that were due by the end of class and placed them on Señor Ascencio's desk. Back at my seat, I worked on a zine for the rest of the period. I was putting away my supplies when a hand snatched the zine from my desk.

"What's this?"

Selena held it between two fingers like it had cooties.

"Give that back!" I said through gritted teeth. I lunged for it, but she took a few steps out of my reach.

"Is this your little diary?" she asked. "It's so cute."

I jumped out of my seat and grabbed for the zine again.

Selena shot me a wicked grin and held the zine behind her back.

"If you don't give that back to me, you're going to be sorry," I warned.

"¿Hay algún problema?" Señor Ascencio asked, looking over in our direction.

Selena tossed the zine back onto my desk. "No, Señor Ascencio," she said sweetly.

"You shouldn't leave your diary lying around, María Luisa," Selena said. She shot daggers at me with her eyes. I gave her the evil eye right back and gathered my things quickly before she had a chance to grab anything else. "Don't touch my things again." My ears burned even more.

"Or what?" Selena asked. She waited a few seconds before walking away.

I really didn't know what I would do. I couldn't remember having had an enemy since kindergarten, when Katie Austen took a crayon and drew mustaches on all the pictures of Grandma Beetle in my copy of *Just a Minute*. I was so mad, I tattled on her when I saw her take two graham crackers during snack time. But that was as far as our feud went. At least then I knew what we were fighting about. But with Selena, it wasn't as easy as crayons and graham crackers. I didn't know what I'd done to make her not like me.

Chapter 11

"Hey, will you sign my petition?"

My language arts class had library orientation, and in the last few minutes we got to check out books from Mr. Baca, our school librarian. I stood in line at the circulation counter waiting my turn.

The girl who spoke to me held a clipboard and wore a serious expression. She had a face full of freckles and the reddest hair I'd ever seen, pulled up into a sloppy, lopsided bun on top of her head. The girl's jacket, an old army one, was covered in pins and patches. There was a rainbow flag, a peace sign, and a pin that said I READ BANNED BOOKS.

"What's it for?" I asked, sliding my book farther down the circulation counter. She moved along with me.

"Better choices in the cafeteria," she said, putting the

clipboard on the counter next to me. "Do we want another school year of lukewarm mac and cheese and oversteamed veggies?"

"Don't forget the unidentifiable blobs," I added.

"Exactly," she said, holding out a pen to me. "You know what I'm talking about."

I took the pen and signed my name on the next available line. She'd only gotten eight signatures.

"How many do you need?" I asked, tapping the petition.

"Mr. Jackson said I should get as many as I can, no max. But I'm aiming for *at least* a hundred."

"You've got a ways to go," I said.

"Don't I know it? I'm Ellie, by the way." Her serious look softened with a smile.

"I'm Malú," I said. "I'm sure you'll get plenty of signatures. It is school lunch we're talking about."

"I think so too," Ellie said.

"So do those petitions really work?"

"Doesn't hurt to try," Ellie said. "My grandma's an old activist, and she always says to me that it's important for us kids to have a voice. Plus, being involved in school looks good on college applications, right?"

I nodded even though I had no idea what she was talking about. We were in the seventh grade, and I wasn't exactly thinking about college yet.

"You should make a petition for a less strict dress code," I said. "I'd sign that."

"Not a bad idea," Ellie said. "But one petition at a time. Next up is a petition to get a daily fifteen-minute break in the morning. You know, so our brains can refresh between classes."

"That sounds like a good idea," I said.

"Anyway, I should probably grab a few more signatures before the bell rings," Ellie said, adjusting her backpack.

"All right, everyone, it's about that time," Mr. Baca called from behind the circulation desk, pointing at the clock. My first week of school was over, and that meant about a hundred and three weeks to go. But who's counting?

"Be sure to grab the flyer for our Fall Fiesta on your way out." He pointed to a stack of green papers on the counter. "It's got the talent show audition date and the art show deadline, so if you're interested in either of those, you should give it a read."

"Thanks again," Ellie said, waving her clipboard.

"Sure, good luck." I watched as she walked up to another girl in our class, her red bun shaking and threatening to topple over as she talked enthusiastically about cafeteria food. Maybe not everyone at Posada was so bad after all.

Chapter 12

The green Fall Fiesta flyer was burning a hole in my backpack when I walked up to our building. But I'd have to wait to reread it because our neighbor, Señora Oralia, was sitting on a rocker on the porch. The sound of a woman's voice, kind of mournful, almost like a wounded animal, filled the air. Goose bumps crawled up my arms. Señora Oralia looked up from what she was doing when I opened the gate.

"Ven, niña." She motioned for me to join her. "You want a snack?"

I really just wanted to go to my room, but Mom would have said that was rude, so I dropped my bag on the floor and sat on the porch swing.

"Cookie?" she asked, pointing to the package of wafer cookies on the table next to her.

Señora Oralia was crocheting something yellow and fluffy. She had an assortment of items on a side table, including a mug of coffee, a small CD player, a few CDs, and . . . a brand-new roll of toilet paper?

"Thank you," I said, and took a cookie. I bit into the thin, crispy outside, and powdery crumbs fell onto my shirt.

"When I was a little girl in Mexico, there were flowers everywhere that same color," Señora Oralia said, pointing to my Day-Glo fuchsia leggings. "Es un color bonito."

Dad said that while a lot of great music came from the eighties, there were a lot of not-so-great things too, like Ronald Reagan and Day-Glo fashion. This was one thing we didn't agree on.

I wore the leggings under a pair of cutoff shorts since I couldn't wear them as bottoms, but Principal Rivera stopped me in the hall between fourth and fifth period and told me cutoff shorts were not allowed either. I asked her if that was in the dress code, not to be a smart aleck but because I didn't remember seeing cutoffs listed. But she ignored my question and told me not to wear them again.

"I like it too," I said. Mom had told me I looked like a "penniless street urchin" before I left for school. You'd be surprised the many ways your mom can insult you when she's an English professor. Nothing I wore was señorita enough for her. I'd decided that Mom and Principal Rivera would probably be best friends if they ever met.

"Who are you listening to?" I asked.

"This is Lola Beltrán," Señora Oralia said. "¡La grande!"

"It sounds really sad," I said.

"Pues, sí. Life is sad, ¿no?"

"Truth, Señora Oralia," I said, finishing my cookie and brushing crumbs off my lap.

"Eh, you're too young to agree," she said, waving me away with her needle. "What do you have to be sad about, niña?"

"I wish I didn't have to move," I said, wondering why adults always thought kids had it so easy. "I wish I was home."

"Ah, sí, home," she said. "You are sad because you miss it?"

"I do."

"What's important is that we keep going. That's how we survive," Señora Oralia said, making a fist like a boxer. "You keep looking back and you get stuck in the past."

"It's not the past," I said. "I *am* going back."

"¿Sí, cuándo?"

"In two years," I said in a whisper, realizing how ridiculous I sounded.

"Two years? ¡Híjole!" Señora Oralia said. "You're going to get tired of waiting."

"Yeah," I said. "It already feels like forever."

"So you have more than one home," Señora Oralia said with a shrug. "That's not a bad thing. Some people don't have any."

"I guess," I said.

"Besides," she went on, "you have your—¿cómo se dice? Your toys? Phone and computer. Like you never left."

"It's not the same," I said.

"Bueno, things could always be worse, ¿no?"

Why did adults always say stuff like that? As if thinking about a worse situation was really going to make you feel better? Señora Oralia was obviously not going to sympathize with me so I changed the subject.

"What are you making?" I asked.

"A cover. Para el toilet paper."

She held up what looked like a frilly Civil War–era skirt for me to see.

"A toilet paper cover?"

"Sí, niña," she said, as if it was the most obvious thing.

On the table next to the plate of wafers was a creepy-looking doll with peach-colored skin and a head of big curly black hair. Instead of legs, her torso tapered into what looked like a short baton. One fat, round, rubbery leg. I shuddered.

I picked up the stack of CDs and read through the names. Some of them were familiar, stuff Mom listened to when she was in a SuperMexican mood.

The Lola Beltrán CD had a photo of a woman with a massive lacquered bun and long spider-leg eyelashes. Her head was tilted back slightly, and she held her hands out in a theatrical gesture. Her long fingers ended in red-polished nails.

"Do you like ranchera music?" Señora Oralia asked. "Does your mami play it for you?"

"She plays it sometimes," I said.

I stacked the CDs back into place neatly.

"Take them," Señora Oralia said.

"Oh, no, I couldn't."

"It's not rock and roll, but it's good music," she said, and let out a raspy chuckle that made it sound like she was laughing at her own little inside joke.

I wondered what Señora Oralia knew about rock and roll. I pulled the Lola Beltrán CD from the top of the pile.

"I'll just borrow this one," I said, not wanting to be rude. "And I'll bring it back right away."

Señora Oralia nodded. "And this is for you and your mami," she said. "A housewarming gift."

I watched as she pulled the crocheted dress onto the creepy doll. She picked up the roll of toilet paper and placed the stumpy doll leg into the center of the cardboard tube. Then she fixed the bottom of the dress until there was no sign of a roll of toilet paper lurking underneath.

"¿Ves?"

She twirled the doll and its frilly dress like it was a debutante.

"Oh, wow," I said. "Uh, thank you."

I took the doll and toilet paper. I didn't know anything about housewarming gifts, but this definitely had to be one of the stranger ones.

"And don't forget this," she said.

Señora Oralia removed the Lola Beltrán CD from the CD player and handed it to me. She popped in another disc before picking up her crochet needle again. I headed inside as a deep male voice sang another sad song.

In my room, I pulled the green sheet out of my backpack and finally got to read it again. Fall Fiesta was an annual fund-raiser carnival at Posada. Food and fun for the whole family, the flyer announced. But the most exciting part, the part I focused on, was toward the bottom. There would be a talent show, and performers were invited to audition. I felt a fountain of hope bubbling up as I read the words out loud one more time: *musical acts welcome*. I couldn't wait to see what kind of cool bands would play. And maybe I'd even have a chance to find my people there.

SEÑORITA
GERMS

WHAT ARE LITTLE GIRLS MADE OF?

sugar

GOOD

neat

helper

sweet

SMILE

PRETTY

NICE

happy

Define DREAM

YOURSELF

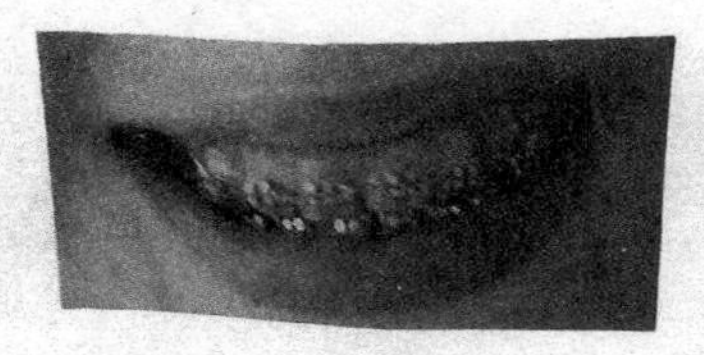

WARNING

MODERN GIRL!

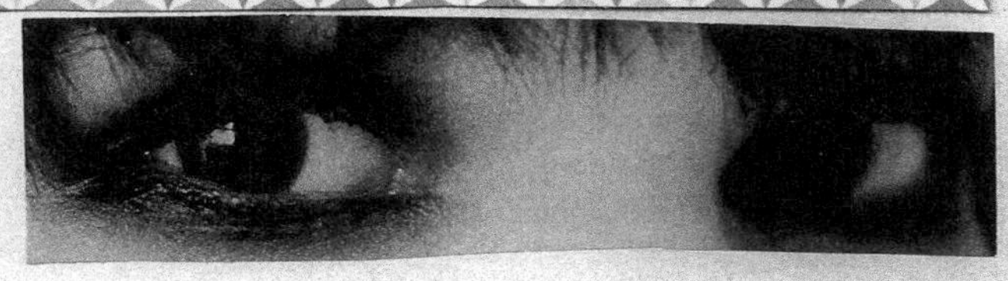

BOLD

SMART

SMELLY

STRONG

ELECTRIC

Cool

SWEATY

CONFIDENT

EXTRAORDINARY

POLY

STYRENE

Her real name was Marianne Elliott-Said, and she's one of my favorite . . .

PUNK SEÑORITAS!

- When she was 18 she saw a punk band play and decided she could do it too!
- She formed the X-Ray Spex in 1977. Their album was "GermFree Adolescents."
- She believed that punk is about what you DO!
- She sang about social issues like the environment and criticized beauty standards!
- She was a vegetarian!
- She wore clothes made out of plastics, mismatched socks, Day-Glo, and braces.

DON'T
3
MESS
WITH
LA DAMA

M

Chapter 13

Before Mom could pack our whole Saturday with boring "cultural events," I asked if I could do homework at Calaca. I had no plans to do any actual work, though. I just wanted to hang out at the only place in Chicago that I liked besides the library. Mom agreed to let me go so long as I texted her as soon as I got there.

Inside Calaca, I walked up to the counter and looked at the selection of pan dulce while I waited for someone to come over. The whooshing of the milk steamer and a banging noise came from behind the espresso machine. A dark head of hair peeked out over the top.

"Dang it!" The person emerged and placed a green mug on the counter in front of me.

"What does this look like to you?" It was the blue-haired

kid who'd been in the auditorium with me on the first day of school. Except his hair was now black.

I looked down at the blob of milk foam floating on the coffee's surface. I knew there was a right answer, but I wasn't sure what it was.

"Umm . . ."

"It's supposed to be a tulip," he said.

"That's what I was going to say."

"Liar," the boy said. "This is so frustrating. I'll never get it."

He took a sip of the coffee before emptying the mug into the sink.

"You wanna order something?"

I looked at the chalkboard menu hanging behind him.

"Can I get a concha?" I asked. "And a Café Olé. Hold the art, please."

"No need to rub it in," he said.

"Sorry." I smiled at him to let him know I was just joking. "Hey, you had blue hair, right? On the first day of school?"

With a square of waxy bakery paper, the boy pulled out a concha frosted with pale yellow sugar and placed it on a plate in front of me.

"That's me," he said, touching his hair. "You had the raccoon eyes."

"They weren't raccoon eyes," I said with a frown. "They were punk eyes, duh."

The boy laughed and slid over to the espresso machine to make my drink.

"Aren't you kind of young to have a job?" I asked.

"I'm thirteen," the boy said. "When my grandfather was my age, he had dropped out of school, crossed the border, and was supporting his family. So, no."

"You sound like my mom with your sad Mexican story," I said.

"You get those too?" He laughed. "Anyway, I don't really have a choice since my parents own the place. Free child labor and all, you know?"

"Wait," I said. "*You're* José?"

"Joe," he said. "How'd you know my name?"

"I met your mom," I said. "And your grandma's my neighbor."

"Did Bueli make you one of her famous toilet paper covers yet?"

I nodded.

"She makes those for everyone," he said, and laughed. "You ain't special."

"Thanks." I thought of the creepy doll that now lived in our bathroom. "Your parents let you work here alone?" I asked, looking around for any sign of an adult presence.

"Yeah, right. They're in the back."

At that moment a loud, heartbroken wail came out of the coffee shop's sound system.

"I know this song," I said. "Your grandma was playing it yesterday."

"Lola Beltrán," Joe said. "Bueli loves Lola Beltrán."

He placed a mismatched ceramic coffee mug and saucer on the counter.

"One café, no art," Joe said with a frown. "I'm really good at those."

Mrs. Hidalgo came out of the back room, her arms full of bags of coffee beans. She wore a brown CALACA COFFEE T-shirt—printed on it was a skeleton holding a mug.

"Art or no art, you make a mean cafecito, m'ijo," she said, easing coffee bags into his arms. "Hi," she said to me, and gave me a big smile. "María Luisa, right?"

"Malú," I said.

I held out a ten-dollar bill for Joe to take.

"It's on the house, Malú," Mrs. Hidalgo said. She waved away my money.

"Really?" I asked. "Thanks."

Mrs. Hidalgo smiled again and started pouring coffee beans into a large grinder.

I picked up my coffee and plate and settled onto a big purple pillow on the floor by the front window. I thought about doing homework like I told Mom I would, but decided to work on a zine instead.

When I finished eating, I placed my plate and mug in the plastic bin for dirty dishes and walked to the wall decorated with album covers.

"You like our wall of fame?"

I turned to find Mrs. Hidalgo nearby, wiping a table.

"Wall of fame?" I asked.

"Sure," she said. "Mexican and Mexican American bands and singers we love. We put them right up there to honor them."

"But Morrissey isn't Mexican," I said, pointing to where

Moz's mopey face looked down on us. Morrissey was the singer of The Smiths, one of Dad's favorite bands, and I knew they were from England.

"That's a joke," Mrs. Hidalgo said with a laugh. "He's an honorary Mexican because he's so popular in Mexico."

"Oh, okay," I said. "That's funny."

"You had a Ramones shirt on the day you came in with your mom, right?"

"Yeah, they're one of my favorite bands," I said.

"You see those guys right there?" She pointed to a record sleeve with a black-and-white image of four guys and THE ZEROS scrawled across the top in hot pink. "They were often called the Mexican Ramones."

"That's weird," I said without thinking.

"What's weird about it?"

I suddenly felt nervous, but Mrs. Hidalgo had a look on her face like she was genuinely interested in why I thought it was strange.

"I don't know," I said. "It just sounds funny. I didn't know there were even Mexican punk bands, I guess."

"Well, technically, they're Mexican American, but sure," she said. "There've been Mexicans in punk for as long as it's been around. There's Alice Bag, the Plugz, the Brat." It sounded like she could go on.

"That's really cool," I said. But *cool* didn't begin to describe what was going through my head. The truth was, back home I always felt like I was the only brown punk in the whole world. Dad understood a lot of things, but I didn't think he could really understand what that was like.

"We're not unicorns in Chicago," Mrs. Hidalgo said, like she could read my thoughts. She winked. "I better get back to work. Next time you're in, I'll play some of these bands for you. Would you like that?"

"Yes," I said, nodding vigorously. "I would *love* that."

"I'll see you soon, then," she said, and headed back into the kitchen as I stood alone with my mind blown.

Chapter 14

On Sunday morning I woke up to the smell of coffee and breakfast cooking. I put on my flip-flops and headed to the kitchen, where Mom whipped eggs in a bowl while a pan of what looked like chorizo sizzled on the stove.

"Good morning, dormilona," Mom said. "Want some coffee?"

"Have I ever said no to coffee?"

"True," Mom said. "I hope this Soyrizo isn't too spicy."

She said the word *Soyrizo* like it was something she still couldn't wrap her brain around.

"I tried to buy some from Mrs. Hidalgo at Calaca, but they were all out. Who knew there was a demand for soy chorizo?" She turned off the burner. "Anyway, she recommended a Mexican place that makes it, so this is as authentic as fake chorizo can be."

"And it's probably going to burn my tongue off, right?"

"Probably," Mom said, handing me a couple of mugs. "I'll get you a glass of milk, too."

"Thanks," I said. As I watched Mom dish eggs and Soyrizo onto two plates, I thought about the family tree assignment for Spanish class. It was looming over me, due tomorrow. Dad always says you have to know when to ask for help, and as much as I dreaded asking Mom, I knew I couldn't do it alone.

"Mom, can you help me with this family tree assignment?"

"Of course," she said a little too eagerly. She placed a plate in front of me and sat down. "When should we work on it?"

"How about now?" I asked. "It's due tomorrow, so I don't have much of a choice."

"Don't sound too excited about it, Malú," Mom said, digging into her breakfast.

I went to my room and grabbed my Spanish notebook and a pen.

"I need at least two generations, not counting me," I said.

"That's it?" Mom asked, sounding disappointed.

"Let's see," I said. "I need full names, and places and dates of birth and death."

Mom held a bottle of hot sauce over her plate, and I watched as she tapped little orange drops across her eggs.

"Okay, well, your abuelo Refugio Morales was born in Morelos in the state of Coahuila in 1936 and died in Anaheim, California, in 2010."

"Slow down," I said. "How do you spell that?"

Mom spelled Coahuila and then continued.

"Why did he leave Mexico?" It wasn't part of my assignment, but I was still curious.

"He came to the US as part of the Bracero Program," Mom said. "Do you know what that is?"

I shook my head.

"During World War II, when many American men had either gone to war or were working in industries that produced equipment for the war, there was a shortage of farm labor," Mom said. "The US government made arrangements with Mexico to bring in laborers to work on American farms. The program continued for a little while after the war ended. That's when your abuelo came. It was supposed to be temporary, but he never left."

"What kind of work did he do?"

"Mostly picked crops," Mom said. "Sugar beets, figs, strawberries."

"Like, for the supermarkets?" I asked.

Mom nodded.

"Wow," I said. "Real people pick that stuff?"

"Well, who do you think does all that work? Machines?"

I shrugged. To be honest, I'd never thought about it all.

"Most people probably don't think about it," Mom said, as if reading my mind. "But it's hard work."

"I remember that Abuelo used to give me those gummy candies that look like orange slices, and I would suck all the sugar off before eating them," I said.

"You remember that?" she asked. "You were so little."

"And we would sit on that plastic-covered couch and watch the show about the kid who lived inside a barrel."

"You're thinking of *El Chavo del Ocho*." Mom smiled, remembering. "Your abuelo loved to watch comedies. He laughed a lot for someone who had a hard life."

"What about Abuela?" I asked.

"Your abuela Aurelia González de Morales was born in Agua Prieta in the state of Sonora in 1948," Mom said.

"When did she come to the US?"

"She left Mexico and her family when she was sixteen," Mom said.

"What do you mean she left her family?" I asked.

"She came alone," Mom said.

"Alone? But isn't that dangerous?"

Mom shrugged like it was no big deal.

"When she was *sixteen*?" I asked. "Mom, that's, like, four years older than me. How did she do it alone?"

"A lot of people come to this country alone, Malú, not knowing the language," Mom said. "It's not an uncommon story. There might be kids in your school whose families came here under similar circumstances."

This was even more mind-boggling than the thought of my abuelo's hands picking the strawberries I saw in the supermarket. I tried to imagine coming to Chicago alone.

It felt scary. Way scarier than how it felt coming here with Mom.

"Your grandparents worked really hard to build a life in this country," Mom said. "But they were also very proud of where they came from."

I chewed on my pen and thought about my grandparents. Abuelo died when I was little, but before that, when they still lived in Florida, I spent more time with them. Once Mom started her PhD program, we saw them less often. And after Abuelo died, Abuela moved to California, where the rest of Mom's family lived. Being so far away and Mom's busy schedule made it harder for us to go visit. Still, Mom called Abuela every weekend and would force me to grab the phone and say hello. I would hear Mom tell my abuela to speak to me in Spanish, but she never did.

"That's why it's important to me that you learn about where you come from," Mom said.

"I know where I come from, Mom," I said, snapping back into the present.

She looked at me and gave me a sad smile. "There are things you're missing out on that are important," she said.

"Like what?"

"You should be proud to speak Spanish, not embarrassed about it."

"I'm not embarrassed," I said. But like Mom, I didn't really believe that either.

"I guess I don't really have anyone to blame but myself," Mom said.

"Gee, sorry to be so disappointing."

"That's not what I meant, Malú," she said. "You're not disappointing."

"Okay," I said. "Is that why you're always talking about how I dress and how I hate speaking Spanish?"

"Whoa, slow down there."

"Admit it, Mom," I said. "I'm just your weird, unladylike, sloppy-Spanish-speaking, half-Mexican kid."

"Where is all this coming from?" Mom asked.

"You want me to be like you and to be interested in stuff you're interested in," I said. "I'm sorry, but I'm not. I can't help it that I care about animals and don't want to eat them. And it's not my fault I don't like hot sauce or cilantro."

Mom burst out laughing. "Malú, do you think I care that you don't like cilantro or that you're a vegetarian?"

"Of course," I said. "Because *real* Mexicans love cilantro and hot sauce on everything. Especially meat."

"I don't expect you to be like me," Mom said. "I just want you to be proud of who you are. Of *everything* you are."

"I am proud of who I am," I said. "It's you who seems to have the problem. You're just like Selena."

"Selena the Tejano singer?" Mom asked, a puzzled look on her face. "What does she have to do with this?"

"Who?" I asked. "Never mind. You don't understand; you never do. I wish I was with Dad."

I grabbed my notebook and left the kitchen. I almost expected Mom to follow me with more questions or at least to fill me in on this Selena singer, but she didn't.

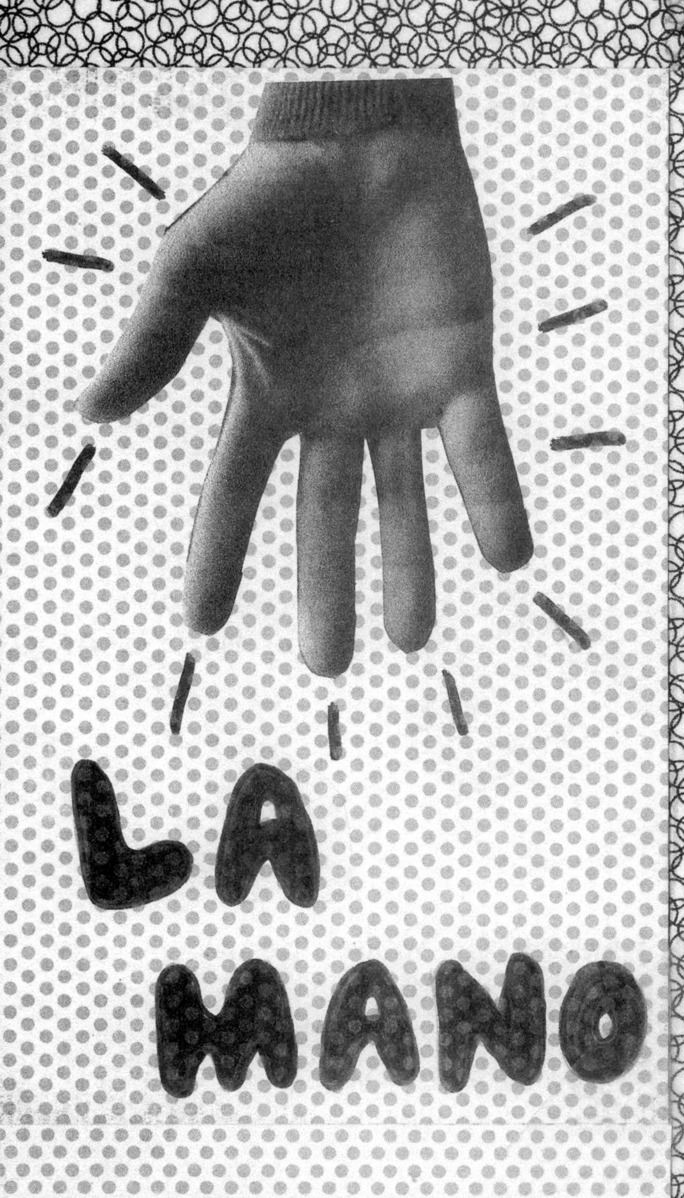
LA
MANO

↳ from the word "brazo"

→ "arm" in Spanish

aguacate

The Mexican Farm Labor Supply Program was known as the BRACERO program

Do you know who picked the strawberries you eat?

About 4.6 million people came from Mexico to work in agriculture. Most of them were in California.

fresa

Started in

1942

BRACEROS experienced . . .

- abuse
- prejudice
- unfair work conditions
- exposure to pesticides (including being fumigated)
- being cheated out of pay and benefits

1964

ended

BRACEROS like my abuelo worked with their arms but also with . . .

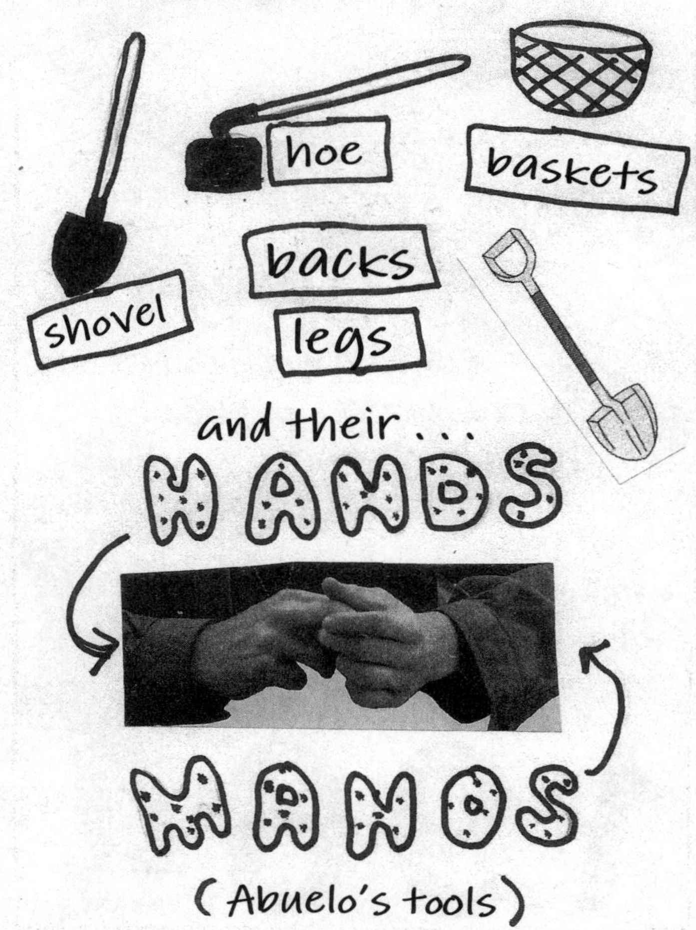

(Abuelo's tools)

I work with
my hands too.
Not in a hard
way like Abuelo.
But we both
CREATE
(My tools)
scissors
paper
glue
stick
markers
and
tape
stack
of old
magazines

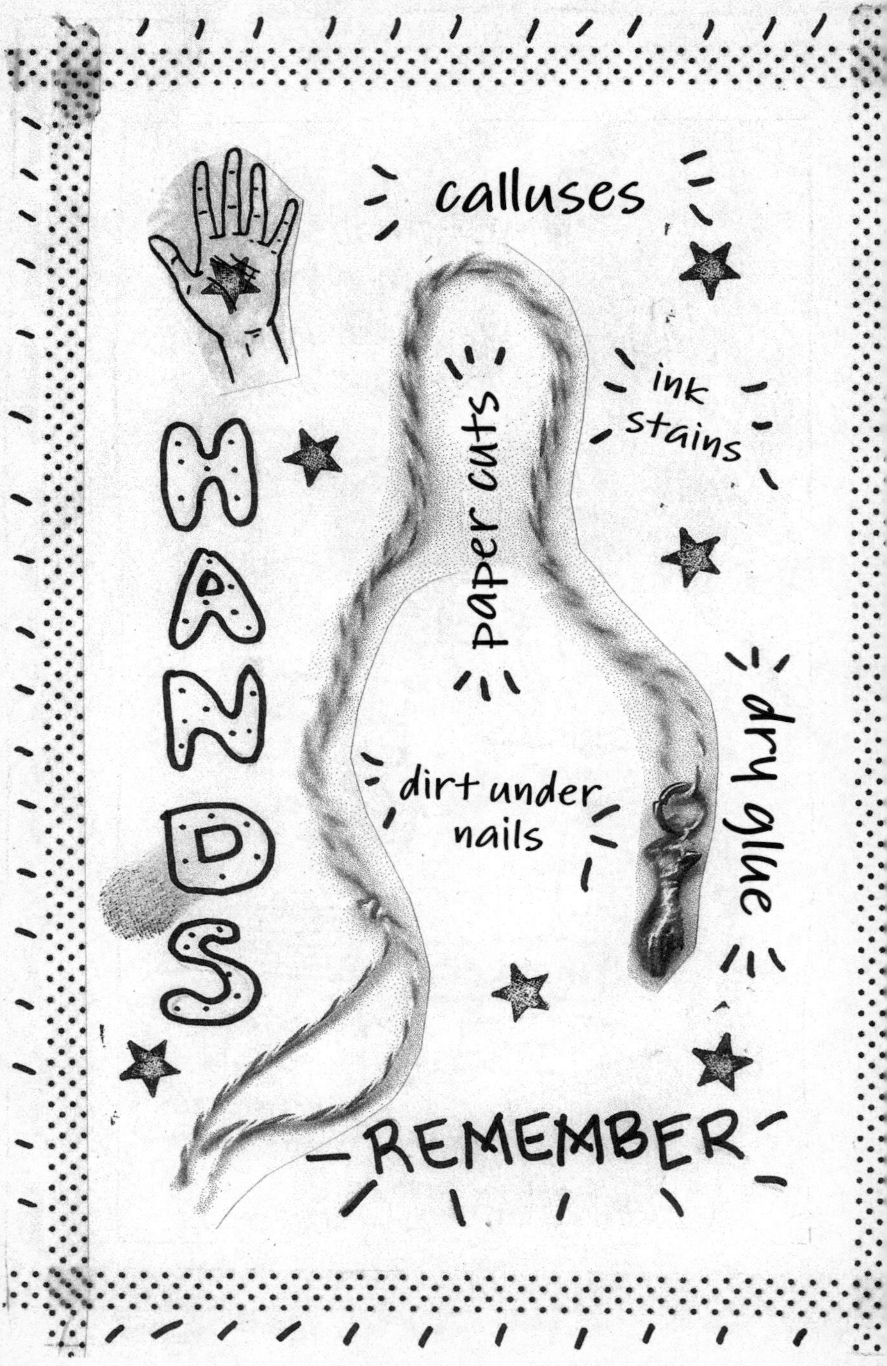

HANDS

calluses

paper cuts

ink stains

dirt under nails

dry glue

REMEMBER

Abuelo and I use our hands to do work. We . . .

DRAW

PULL

PLANT

SOW

CUT

PASTE

REAP

FOLD

MAKE

TEAR

transform

MAGIC
M

Chapter 15

On Monday at back-to-school night I waited for Mom outside homeroom. She finally arrived hauling her many workbags, glasses on top of her head.

"Whew, made it!" she said, giving me a quick hug. "Trains were delayed."

"No time to change, huh?" I asked.

"What are you talking about?"

She had on a blue dress embroidered with colorful flowers, sandals, and a big chunky necklace. Her hair was twisted into a knot and held in place with a pencil. She looked like a college professor version of Frida Kahlo.

"Can't you ever wear anything, you know, normal?"

Mom eyed my outfit in response.

I wore a red corduroy miniskirt, which Principal Rivera subjected to the fingertip test as I hurried to history class, striped tights, my Doc Martens, and a T-shirt Dad had given me. It was gray with a picture of Judy Garland as Dorothy carrying Toto in his basket. It read: TOTO IS MY COPILOT.

"Let's not argue about clothes right now," Mom said. "Where to?"

"Follow me." I led her to the first classroom.

In each room, kids were on their best behavior, while parents read classroom rules taped to walls, inspected titles on bookshelves, and waited for teachers to give quick overviews of what the class would be working on that school year. Listening to Ms. Freedman, the seventh-grade science teacher, describe the spring unit on the solar system reminded me that I was really going to be there for the entire school year. *Two* entire school years. In science terms, the Earth would travel around the sun twice before I would be able to go back home for good.

When we got to Señor Ascencio's classroom, he was at the door, greeting everyone. As we came in, he handed us each a clothespin and our graded family trees to hang on twine that had been strung across the back of the room. I flipped my drawing over and saw an A in red marker on the back.

"An A! Malú, that's great," Mom said. "Can I see?"

I held up the clothespin.

"I'm going to hang it up," I said. "Then you can look at it, okay?"

"Going to make me wait? Fine, I'm going to talk to your teacher."

Mom walked off toward Señor Ascencio, and I headed to the back of the room to hang up my tree. I saw Joe come in, and I waved.

"That's a pretty good drawing," Joe said, walking up.

"Thanks," I said. "When do you have Señor Ascencio's class?"

"Second period," he said.

"So which one is your tree?"

"You really want to see it?" Joe asked.

"Sure," I said. Then, with a grin, I added, "Is it better than your foam tulip?"

"Real funny," Joe replied, frowning. "Over here." I followed him down the row of hanging trees and stopped when he stopped. His tree had a large trunk painted in swirling shades of brown. In the swirls he'd written names and painted what looked like animals: a large cat, tropical birds, an elephant. The trunk split into branches full of soft, feathery bright green leaves where he'd also hidden names.

"Whoa," I said. "It's . . . it's beautiful."

"It's el árbol del Tule. The Tule Tree," he said. I could see pink rushing into his cheeks and ears.

"What's that?" I asked.

"It's this huge super-old tree in Mexico," he said. "I saw it when I was eight. I've never felt so small in my life."

"What are the names in the trunk?"

"Those are all my grandparents and great-grandparents," Joe said. "Me and my parents are up here." He pointed to the leaves.

"I like it," I said. "You're a really good artist."

"Thanks," Joe said. "Watercolors, I can work with. Milk foam, not so much."

Over his shoulder I could see Mom talking to Selena and a woman I assumed was her mother.

"Oh no," I said. "I better go. I'll see ya."

"Yeah, go rescue your mom," Joe said, turning to look. "I should go find mine too."

I left Joe by the hanging trees and hurried over to Mom.

"There you are," Mom said.

"Come look at my tree, Mom." I hoped she'd be so excited to check out my A, she'd want to leave Selena and her mom quickly.

"Don't be rude, María Luisa. Aren't you going to say hello to your friend?" she asked, motioning to Selena. "And this is Selena's mother, Señora Ramirez."

"Hi," I said, giving Señora Ramirez a strained smile while ignoring Selena. "Okay, Mom, let's go. The bell's about to ring."

"Nice to meet you, Señora Morales," Selena said sweetly. "See you later, María Luisa."

"It's Malú," I said, and grabbed Mom's arm. I pulled her away as she said good-bye to Selena and her mother.

"I hate to break this news to you, Mom," I said, "but Selena is not my friend."

"She seems really nice. And did you know she dances huapango? Very impressive."

"Huapa-what?"

"It's a traditional Mexican dance," Mom said. "You

know, Malú, it wouldn't hurt you to make friends."

"I have friends," I said.

"Who?" Mom asked.

A very good question.

"Joe. Mrs. Hidalgo's kid," I said. "One friend is all this girl needs."

Mom rolled her eyes. "Selena's mother runs her own dance school," Mom said. "I've always wanted to learn some traditional Mexican dances."

"That's great, Mom," I said, still trying to move away from the topic of Selena. "Look, there's my tree."

"I told her we'd sign up for a beginners' lesson."

I stopped in my tracks. "We?"

"When will we have this opportunity again?" Mom asked. "I want us to take advantage while we can."

"But I don't want to do it," I said.

"It would be fun for us to do this together, Malú," Mom said. "Think about it: it's just one lesson. Now, where's this tree?"

I pointed to my tree and waited while Mom inspected it and read my essay.

"This is lovely, Malú."

"Thanks," I mumbled, my arms crossed over my chest.

"Are you going to be mad at me now?" she asked.

I wasn't mad; I was furious. And panicking at the thought of having to spend an afternoon outside of school with Selena.

"Nice work on the tree," Mom said. "I wish you would've let me look over your essay before you turned it in."

"I got an A, didn't I?"

My sentences were short, and I spelled everything out exactly as it sounded using the information Mom and Dad had given me. I'd thought about having Mom check over it, but decided against it. I knew it would have given her too much pleasure. Plus, I didn't want to hear her criticize my Spanish. I could picture all the red pen marks on my paper, like I was one of her students.

"I guess you did," Mom said. "But you know I'm happy to help."

"I know, Mom," I said.

"Sounds like you're going to have a great school year."

"Yeah," I said. "The awesomest."

"I need to go to the restroom before we leave," Mom said, ignoring me. "I'll meet you out front."

I was curious to see what grade Selena got on her tree—an A+, probably—so I walked along the back of the room, looking at the trees, in search of it. I noticed that almost all of the locations on the trees were either Chicago or Mexico. Some California and Texas. Mine was the only one with a non-Spanish name. I was probably the only one in this class who couldn't dance a huapa-whatever, too.

When I got to Selena's, I stopped. It looked like she'd done a lot of work on it. There was a printout of a tree image with photos of family members superimposed on branches. At the top was a photo of Selena smiling. The whole thing was printed in color on this fancy, shiny paper.

"Admiring my work?" Selena asked.

"I'm looking at all of them," I said. "Not just yours."

Selena leaned against the back of a chair. “My mom says our family was here before the border,” she said.

“All our families were here before the border, tonta,” Joe said over her shoulder as he walked past.

Selena sucked her teeth and swatted at him. He jumped out of her reach, laughing, and left the room. I wanted to call out for him to not abandon me.

“I hear you might be coming to the studio,” Selena said.

“Not if I can help it,” I replied.

“Yeah, it might be hard for you to get the hang of a Mexican dance,” Selena said. “I'd be nervous too.”

“Whatever,” I said. “You don't know anything about me.”

“You and your mom are so different,” Selena went on. “I guess I'm not surprised.”

My ears started to burn, and all of a sudden I felt hot all over. I had to get out of there, away from Selena. Fast.

“Are you like your dad?” Selena asked. “Is he . . . you know?”

“No, I don't know.”

“Is he a weirdo too?”

I turned away from the hanging trees and left her standing alone. I couldn't believe Mom actually thought Selena and I would ever be friends.

Mom was near the building's entrance, talking to Mrs. Hidalgo, when I found her. I busied myself looking at the announcements on the bulletin board near the door. There were club flyers, the week's lunch menu, even an ad for a student's dog-walking business. And in the middle of it all was the sign-up sheet for the Fall Fiesta talent show auditions. I read down the list of names until I came to Selena Ramirez.

At that moment, Joe walked up to get a drink from the water fountain. "What's your talent?" he asked.

"What's *yours*?"

Joe tried to rub his stomach and pat his head at the same time.

"With talent like that, what are you doing here?" I asked, and laughed. "You should be on the road."

"Harsh," Joe said. "So, you signing up?"

I tapped my finger against Selena's name. "What do you think she's going to do?" I asked. "Dance?"

"She's definitely dancing," Joe said. "That's her thing."

"You play any instruments?" I asked.

"Some guitar, a little piano. But I prefer the visual arts," Joe said. "Why?"

I grabbed the pen that was hanging on a string next to the sign-up sheet and wrote my name on a blank line. Next to it, in parentheses, I wrote the word *band*.

"Because we're starting a band," I said.

Chapter 16

I watched as the lunch ladies slapped food onto trays.

"They're like artists, right?" Joe asked, sliding his tray down. "Like Jackson Pollock in hairnets."

"Who's Jackson Pollock?" I asked, nodding at the green blob a lunch lady offered.

"He was a painter," Joe said. "He worked by dripping and splashing paint on his canvases."

"Who knew you were such an art nerd?" I said.

"I'm a man of many interests, thanks very much," Joe said. "Come on, I told this kid I know named Benny to meet us at my usual table. If you're serious about this band thing, you're going to want to know him too."

The slapping and dripping of food was so mesmerizing that I didn't notice the pile of cilantro the lunch lady dumped on my serving of guacamole until I slid out of line.

"Great," I muttered. Its sickening soapy scent drifted up toward my nose as I nervously followed Joe to his table.

I'd been eating lunch in the library whenever Mr. Baca would let me stick around. I even offered to reshelve books when I was done eating. It was a good way to avoid Selena. Plus, it just felt weird to sit alone in the cafeteria every day.

"Hey, Ben-man," Joe said, and slapped hands with the boy at his table. It was the tall kid I'd met in the lunch line on my first day. "This is María Luisa, dude."

"Malú," I corrected him, and set my tray down across from Benny. "Hi."

"Fan of the orange blob, huh?" Benny asked.

"Yeah, I guess so," I said, looking down at my double serving of sweet potatoes with butter and cinnamon.

"Benny here just joined the school marching band," Joe said. "We used to play together in this kid mariachi group back in the day," Joe said. "I can't believe our moms made us do that. Remember those little suits we had to wear, bro?"

"Still doing it, *bro*," Benny said. He gave Joe a look that said he didn't appreciate him poking fun at the kid mariachi band.

"That's cool," Joe said. "So, not to change the subject, but María Luisa is forming a band for the Fall Fiesta talent show, and I told her you might be interested."

"Is that why I'm here?" Benny asked. "I thought you were missing the little mariachi suits and wanted back in."

Joe gave him a guilty grin.

"What do you play?" I asked. Benny's black instrument case sat on the floor between us.

"Trumpet," Benny said.

"Do you play anything else?" I knew beggars couldn't be choosers, as Mom liked to say, but I had to ask. What the band needed was drums, not trumpet.

"Seriously?" Benny asked, shaking his head.

I started to pull out the tiny cilantro leaves that were ruining my perfectly good guacamole. If you ever want to torture me, just force-feed me cilantro. Mom jokes that it's my diluted Mexican genes that make it taste soapy to me.

"If you don't want those, you can drop them here," Benny said, and pointed to his tray.

I flicked the leaves onto his tray with my plastic spork.

"Auditions are next week," I said. "We don't have a lot of time, so we need to know now."

"Actually, I was thinking of playing with some of the kids from band class," Benny said.

"Come on, old pal," Joe said. "We could use a real musician like you."

Joe gave Benny what I assumed was his sad puppy dog face. I put my palms together, pleading, and smiled hopefully. I didn't know Benny, but I really wanted this band to happen.

Benny looked between me and Joe like we were pathetic then shrugged.

"What's your plan?" he asked.

"Yes!" Joe held out his fists for us to bump. I'd never

bumped fists with anyone, but Benny bumped one, so I did the same.

"Well, I guess we need a name, for starters," I said.

"Ooh, how about los Rudos?" Joe asked. "That's good, right?"

"Yeah," Benny said. "We can wear lucha libre masks like Mil Máscaras and Rey Mysterio."

"Why would we do that?" I asked.

"Dude," Joe said, shaking his head. "Los rudos are the bad guys in wrestling."

"Oh," I said. "I don't know. It probably gets really hot in those masks."

"The Atomic Fireballs," Benny said, holding up a red-hot candy before popping it into his mouth.

"I kind of like that," I said. "It's punky." I opened a notebook and wrote down the names we'd come up with so far.

"Botched Manicure?" Joe asked. "I read it in a magazine at the dentist's office. It sounded gnarly."

"Gross," I said, but I wrote it down anyway.

"What about Dorothy and the Flying Monkeys?" I asked. "Like in *The Wizard of Oz*."

"And I assume we're the flying monkeys?" Joe asked.

He and Benny looked at each other and frowned, but I smiled as I wrote it down, picturing Joe and Benny in those funny little hats and jackets.

We didn't get a chance to move on to the next suggestion because Selena walked up with Diana and a couple of boys in tow. They all wore matching candy necklaces, even the boys. Like a pack of clones that escaped from Willy Wonka's factory.

"Looks like you found your table," she said. "I warned you."

"You always say the nicest things," I said, closing my notebook.

"I saw your name on the audition sign-up for the talent show," Selena said. "I hope you aren't seriously thinking of entering."

"What if we are?" Joe asked.

"We?" Selena asked. "You too, Benny? Are you playing your trompeta?"

"Maybe," Benny said, looking uncomfortable.

"I bet it'll be some kind of weird coconut music, right, María Luisa?"

She winked at me like we were in on a joke together. It was the second time she'd said something about coconuts, and I still didn't get it.

"What are you doing?" Joe asked. "Your tired cucaracha-killing dance?"

Selena pulled off her candy necklace and began playing with it, twisting it into a cat's cradle. "You seem to have forgotten that you were into that 'cucaracha-killing dance' too. Before you turned into a coconut."

"It's true," Benny said, laughing. "Joe could stomp like nobody's business."

Joe punched Benny in the arm.

"You guys are no fun," Selena said, pouting.

"Move along then, Cantinflas," Joe said. I remembered Cantinflas was one of the Mexican comedians my abuelo liked to watch. He had a funny little mustache that looked like it was drawn on with a pencil. I giggled at the thought of Selena with a pencil-drawn mustache over her lips.

Selena put the palm of her hand in Joe's face.

"Later, weirdos," she said, then turned and walked off with her friends.

"Why'd you let her call you a coconut, María Luisa?" Joe asked.

"I don't even know what that means," I said. "A coconut?"

Joe and Benny looked at each other and laughed.

"Brown on the outside, white on the inside," Benny said. "Get it?"

I could feel my ears burn. Suddenly the joke made sense.

"Forget her," Joe said, swatting in her direction. "I'm hyped about this band. We can practice in my basement. My mom has stuff in there from her band days we can probably use."

"Don't we need a fourth person?" Benny asked. "Right now we're a three-person band."

"I'll play guitar," Joe said. "María Luisa, you're good to sing, right?"

"Malú," I said. "It's Malú." I would have felt more annoyed that Joe kept calling me by my full name if not for the news that I'd have to have to sing. What had I gotten myself into? "Yeah . . . I guess."

"I can play bass," Benny said. "I mean, I don't know how to, but maybe I can figure it out."

"We need a drummer, too," I said.

"Don't forget a name and a song," Joe said.

"And probably some skill," Benny added.

"Thanks for the reminders," I said. I bit into my quesadilla, wondering if this would be too much work for a group with zero experience.

"Hey, why don't we mess with Selena and call ourselves the Coconuts?" Joe asked.

He and Benny cracked up, but I wrote it down in my notebook. I chewed on my cap.

"What about instead of the Coconuts, we're the Co-Co's?" I asked.

"I was kidding," Joe said. "And no offense, but that's pretty awful."

"No, it's not," I said. "It's short for coconuts. But it's also like the Go-Go's. You know, that band from the eighties?"

Benny and Joe looked at me like they had no idea what I was talking about.

"Ask your mom about the Go-Go's," I said with a sigh. "She'll know. Anyway, coconuts is supposed to be an insult, right? So we use it our own way and then it isn't. That's totally punk rock."

"Whatever," Joe said with a shrug. "Let's just go with that."

"Really?" I asked. "You should care more. It's our band name!"

"Like you said," Joe went on. "We don't have a lot of time to waste."

"I like the Co-Co's," Benny said. "Even though I'm not a coconut myself." He laughed.

I looked down at the page in my notebook, then at Joe.

"So, we're the Co-Co's?"

He cupped his hands around his mouth like a megaphone.

"Señoras y señores, put your hands together for the Co-Co's!"

We all laughed. We had a name, and by the time the bell rang, we had a plan to meet at Joe's the next day after school.

As I walked to class I spotted Ellie's red messy bun and pin-covered army jacket ahead of me. I got an idea and quickened my pace until I caught up to her.

"Hi," I said. "How's your petition going?"

"Oh, hey," Ellie said. "It's going pretty well. I've got one hundred and thirteen signatures. But I think I can get more before I present it to Principal Rivera."

"That's really cool," I said. "Can I ask you a question?"

"What's up?"

"Do you play any instruments?"

"Let me think." Ellie looked up, pretending to think about the answer. "No. Okay, wait. That's a lie. I played the recorder in fifth grade."

"Recorder, huh?" I said, thinking of how that could help the band. "Okay, well, do you *want* to be in a band?"

"Why would I do that?" she said, and laughed. "I just said I don't play an instrument."

"This is a totally separate question," I said. "Forget the instrument part. Band?"

"Uhh, I don't know," Ellie said. "I'm kind of busy."

"You've got a guitar pin on your bag, so you must like music, right?"

I followed her down the hall even though we were going in the opposite direction from my next class.

"Well, yeah, I like music. That doesn't mean I want to be in a band," she said. She glanced at her phone. "Sorry. I'm going to be late."

I knew I was about to lose her, so I said the only thing I thought might make her think twice.

"It would look good on a college application," I said. "Right?"

Ellie stopped walking and looked at me like maybe she was actually considering it.

"I'm putting together a band for the talent show," I said. "We need a drummer."

"I can't play drums," she said, and waved. We'd reached her classroom, and she turned to walk inside. "Good luck with your band."

"Wait," I said. "What if I help you get signatures for your petition?"

Ellie turned around.

"Yeah?"

"I help you, you help me?" I asked.

"How will I be any help to you?" Ellie asked. "For the hundredth time, I don't know how to play any instruments."

I thought about what Dad always said. *You think every*

musician that's ever lived had formal lessons? If you want to do it, you find a way.

"You'll learn," I said. "We'll help you."

"We?"

"The band," I said.

"By next week?" Ellie looked dubious.

"Yeah," I said. "Don't worry about it. You in?"

Ellie looked at me like she was thinking about something else. Maybe which Ivy League school's offer she would accept.

"Okay, thirty signatures," she said. "That will bring me closer to one fifty. Then we have a deal." She unzipped her backpack and pulled out her clipboard. I took the signature sheet Ellie held out for me.

"Just thirty?" I asked. "No problem."

Chapter 17

Mom sat at the kitchen table with her familiar semester-preparation spread. Her laptop was open, and there were papers and books everywhere.

"Whatever you do, do not touch the sticky notes," she said when I sat down. I began stacking her books by size.

"I wouldn't dream of messing with your system, Mom."

"You'd better not. How was school?"

"School was school," I said, placing the last and smallest book on top of the pile.

Mom looked away from her screen. "I don't appreciate the attitude," she said.

"I'm helping this girl Ellie get signatures for a petition," I said, checking my tone.

"That's great," Mom said. "What's it for?"

"Fewer blobs, more real food in the cafeteria."

"I'm glad you're getting involved, Malú," Mom said, ignoring the fact that I'd just told her the school was feeding us blobs. She smiled a smile of relief. Like my helping with a petition meant I was settling into my new life and everything was fine. "How's language arts? What are you reading?"

Mom and I didn't seem to have a whole lot in common, but we both loved to read.

"*The Outsiders,*" I said.

"I love *The Outsiders,*" Mom said. "Such a great book."

"It's okay." I wasn't about to tell her that it was more than okay. That I understood the way Ponyboy often felt mismatched too.

"Any authors of color on your reading list?"

"What color?" I asked. "There might be a purple author on it."

"Very funny."

I shrugged. I knew I was getting on her nerves. Mom taught US Latino literature in the English department, so sniffing out "authors of color" was one of her SuperMexican superpowers.

"There should be," she said. "We're in one of the most diverse cities in the country."

I let out a pretend snore.

"Do you have to be such a grouch?" Mom asked, gathering her things. "I'm glad we're here and that you're surrounded by people from all kinds of backgrounds. Not to mention all the Spanish you get to hear and study in school every day. I hope some of it will stick."

"Why?" I asked. "So I won't be such a weirdo coconut?" I didn't mean to say the coconut part, but it came out before I could stop myself.

"I *mean,* so that maybe you'll want to speak it," Mom said, closing her laptop. "What's this coconut business about?"

"It's nothing," I said. "And for your information, I can speak Spanish just fine. I *choose* not to."

"Well, that makes me sad," she said. "I wish you thought of it as a part of who you are, that's all."

"You mean who you wish I was."

"I hate that we're having this conversation when I have to leave for class, Malú," Mom said, glancing at her watch before giving me her concerned parent look. "Let's finish this later, okay?"

Talking about this again with Mom was nowhere on my list of things to do. What did Mom know about the coconut life anyway?

"Anything else going on at school that I should know about?" Mom asked as she shoved books into a large canvas bag.

This would have been the moment to tell her about the band and the talent show. But I knew there was no way I could. It would just be one more thing for her to disapprove of.

"Nope," I said. "Nada."

"There's a quiche in the fridge, and I told Señora Oralia that you'll be here alone."

"Mom, I can take care of myself," I said. "Besides,

Señora Oralia is about a hundred years old. I should be taking care of her."

"That is so nice of you to offer to check in on her," Mom said. "I bet she'd like the company."

"I wasn't offering," I said, following Mom to the door.

Mom smiled and planted a kiss on my forehead. "Oh, before I forget," she said. "I signed us up for the intro dance class on Saturday morning."

"You aren't serious," I said. My heart pounded like there was a bird trapped inside trying desperately to get out.

"Of course I am," Mom said. "I told you about it at back-to-school night, remember?"

"No," I said, shaking my head. "You told me to think about it."

"Well, I let Señora Ramirez know that we're both coming," she said. "It'll be fun. Now, lock up behind me."

The little bird in my heart stopped flapping its wings. I knew there would be no discussion. This was one cultural adventure I wasn't getting out of.

After Mom left, I pulled out my notebook and tried to think of some songs to bring to our first band meeting. If we got into the talent show, we would have to perform in front of the entire school, in front of parents, and in front of Selena. We didn't have a song or a real drummer. I could never bring myself to sing into the microphone at record store shows. How were we ever going to play as a band?

I got that out-of-control feeling like when you're on a roller coaster, strapped in, and you realize it's too late to get off the ride. All you can do is close your eyes, hang on tight, and wait for it to end. So I called Dad because I knew he could at least slow down the roller coaster for me.

"Ramones songs are easy to learn," he said. In true Dad fashion, he had all the answers. Or at least some of them. "Besides, everyone will be so entranced by the lead singer, they won't even notice if the band is good or not."

"I don't know," I said. "I've never performed in front of a crowd of people."

"I'm proud of you for trying something that scares you."

"Dad," I said. "Do you know what a coconut is?"

"Only the key ingredient in my favorite candy bar," he answered. "Why?"

"No, like, if someone calls you a coconut," I said. "It means you're brown on the outside and white on the inside." I told him about our band's name.

"That's pretty clever," Dad said. "And subversive. It works."

"I guess."

"What's the problem, then?"

I thought about Dad's question. What *was* the problem? Why did it bother me so much that Selena called me a coconut?

"I don't know," I said. "It makes me feel like there's something wrong with who I am."

"There's nothing wrong with you, Malú," Dad said. "You can't let what other people think about you bother you; you'll never be happy if you do. Turning an insult into something you embrace is a good way of empowering yourself."

"Yeah, sticks and stones," I mumbled, though I wasn't feeling very powerful at that moment.

"And as far as the dancing goes, if you inherited my moves, the lesson will be a piece of cake."

"You're a terrible dancer, Dad," I said.

"Exactly. Step on your mom's toes for an hour, and that will be the last dance lesson you take!"

"Good plan," I said, and laughed.

"Besides, showing up and making the effort goes a long way," he said. "Your mom will be less likely to give you a hard time about it if you at least try."

"You're right," I said.

"Hey, have you checked out the record store I told you about?" Dad asked.

"Not yet," I said. "But I will soon."

I couldn't tell Dad that we'd been right near the store and I'd chosen not to go because it was too hard. I knew what he would say. Not doing something because it's hard *isn't* punk.

I lifted my pillow and counted the worry dolls. All present and accounted for. "Punks don't dance," I said to their little faces before placing the pillow back over them.

A HANDBOOK FOR COCONUTS

(No. Not this kind!)

Welcome to the OFFICIAL handbook for coconuts.

A "COCONUT" is a mean name for someone who doesn't meet expectations. It means you are

Ridiculous, right? What does that really mean? Why can't we just

BE?!

You May Be a Coconut If . . .

☐ You find yourself inside a delicious candy bar.

Or If You're Brown on the Outside But . . .

☐ Your Spanish is terrible. You have no idea where the accent marks go.

´ this guy

~ this guy

wrong!

No Problemo!

coconut

?

coconut coconut coconut

☐ Spicy food turns you into a fire-breathing monster.

☐ Cilantro tastes like a bar of soap.

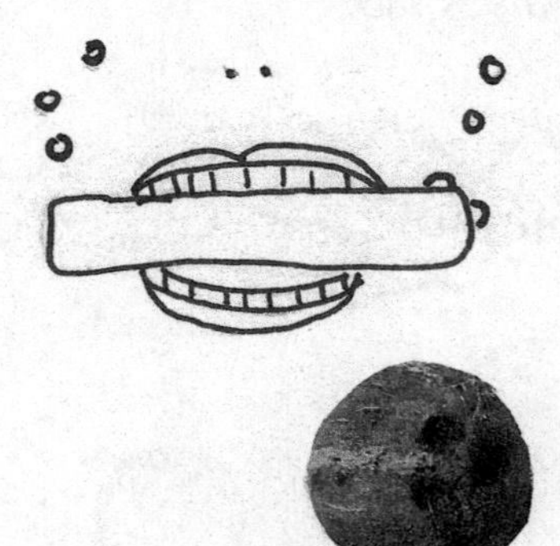

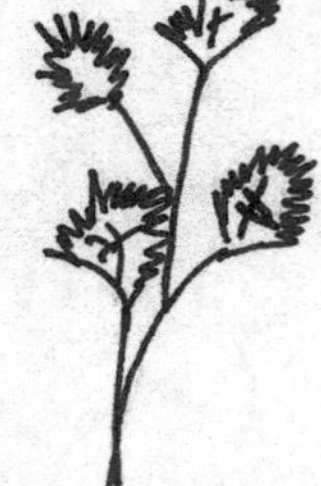

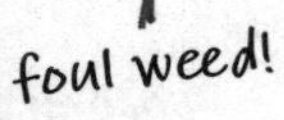

If these describe YOU then you too might be a . . . COCONUT! (cue dramatic music)

QUESTIONS YOU MAY HEAR A LOT!

- ☐ What are you?
- ☐ Where are you from?

- ☐ How come you never speak Spanish?
- ☐ Why don't you like ______?
- ☐ What kind of ______ person doesn't eat ______?

CONGRATULATIONS!

You are officially a member of the

SISTER (BROTHER) HOOD OF COCONUTS

Clip out your membership card and show it at restaurants so that you don't have to embarrass yourself by telling them to hold the cilantro.

SISTER (BROTHER) HOOD
OF
COCONUTS
cilantro-ruiner of tacos
enemy of guacamole
(your name)
Never
(expiration date)
MEMBERSHIP CARD
M

Chapter 18

Joe's place was a two-story brick house with a small, unfenced front yard. Before I rang the doorbell, I sent Mom a text to remind her I was hanging at Joe's. I'd told her we were working on a school project, which was technically true. Mrs. Hidalgo opened the door wearing a pink ruffled apron over her jeans and T-shirt. The apron matched the stripe in her hair.

"Malú, come on in," she said. "Good to see you again."

"Hi, Mrs. Hidalgo," I said.

The sweet smell of vanilla and powdered sugar filled the air when I stepped into the Hidalgos' house. I imagined it must be what the gingerbread house in the forest smelled like to Hansel and Gretel, yummy and inviting. But unlike the gingerbread house, the Hidalgos' home felt safe. There was no danger lurking. Unless you counted the possibility of my band plan completely falling apart.

"Go ahead and put your bag down," Mrs. Hidalgo said. "Joe's pretty excited about the band."

"Me too," I admitted.

"Well, I offered Joe my services if the Co-Co's need them."

"Thanks," I said. "I'm pretty sure we're going to need help."

"I'm baking, but I'm almost done. Give me a holler when you need me," she said. "They're in the basement, first door down the hallway."

I gave her a little wave and headed in the direction of the basement.

As I walked down the stairs, my stomach flip-flopped like a fish out of water. What if the band was a big failure? What if I couldn't find the nerve to sing? What if Ellie decided not to show up after all? I'd left a note in her locker with Joe's address.

"Hey, Malú," Benny said when I reached the bottom of the stairs.

To my surprise, Ellie was already there. She sat with Joe and Benny on the carpeted floor. There was a drum kit set up, as well as a few acoustic and electric guitars. Against one wall were record crates. I felt like I was at Dad's place, back home again.

"Oh good, you're here," I said, trying not to sound too relieved.

"Yeah, I can't believe it either," she said, shaking her head.

"Do you guys know each other?" I asked as I fished the petition out of my bag.

"We do now," Joe said.

"Benny's in my science class," Ellie added. "Now, hand over my thirty signatures."

I found the sheet and placed it in her outstretched palm.

"So . . . it's more like twenty-seven signatures," I said. "Is that okay? 'Cause we really need you."

The only way I'd even gotten that many was by asking Mr. Baca for permission to tape the petition to the circulation desk in the library.

Ellie looked at the names on the sheet. I waited, afraid she'd say no deal and leave.

"Fine," she said, adding the page to her clipboard. "Did you guys sign this yet?" She held it out to Benny and Joe.

"Yeah, twice," Joe said, and laughed.

"Only one signature counts," Ellie said with a frown.

Joe shrugged.

"So you're really in?" I asked.

"Sure," Ellie said. "I can't play drums, but I do have my own drumsticks." She pulled the sticks out of her bag and held them up. "I asked my mom to take me shopping for these. I'm actually excited to use them."

"Wait, you mean you brought us a drummer who can't play drums?" Joe asked.

"Punk rock is all about DIY," I said. "That stands for do-it-yourself, and that includes learning how to play an instrument." I smiled at Ellie. I was secretly happy to have another girl in the band. "Watch some videos, listen to the song a bunch, and you'll be playing in no time."

"You're nuts, María Luisa," Joe said, shaking his head.

I made a face at Joe. "Besides, my dad says Ramones songs are easy to play," I said. "Listen to this."

I pulled up a song on my phone and hit play. When the song ended, everyone looked at me like I was as nuts as Joe claimed.

"That doesn't sound easy," Ellie said.

"Your mom offered to help us." I turned to Joe. "Can you ask her?"

"Oh man, she would love that too much," Joe said. "No way, dude."

"Come on," I pleaded. "We need help."

"Then you go ask her."

"Fine, I will," I said. I stood and stomped up the stairs.

I followed the sound of banging metal and found Mrs. Hidalgo crouched in front of the oven, pulling a cookie sheet out with a mitt-covered hand.

"It smells really good in here," I said.

"Hey, I'm making vegan polvorones," she said. "Mexican wedding cookies." She pointed to a tray on the counter. "Try one."

I picked up a powdered cookie and bit into it.

"Well?"

"It's good," I said, leaning against the counter. "I think I've had these before. Not vegan, though."

"Just trying to add some options at the coffee shop," Mrs. Hidalgo said.

"Need any help?" I asked.

"I won't turn down help, but aren't you needed in the basement?"

"Actually, I came to get you," I said, and gave her a nervous grin. "We need *your* help."

"Okay then, how about you help me finish up here?" Mrs. Hidalgo said. "Take each cookie and roll it in the powdered sugar. Then place it on the cookie sheet." She slid a metal bowl full of snowy sugar in front of me.

I turned on the warm water and soaped up my hands. As Mrs. Hidalgo and I worked, I tried to get a closer look at the tattoos on her arms without being too obvious.

On her right forearm, she had a cluster of pink and orange flowers that looked like balls of tiny petals. Kind of like something you'd draw with a Spirograph, repeating the pattern of tiny petals over and over. Below that, on her wrist, she had two sets of initials written in black script inside an anatomical heart. On her other arm, there was the image of a girl.

The girl looked like Pippi Longstocking, except she had black braids sticking up on either side of her head. Instead of Pippi's white freckled face, the tattoo girl's face was brown and round with thick lips and a wide nose. She sort of resembled one of those huge stone Olmec heads. She wore striped socks like Pippi and what looked like an embroidered Mexican dress, the kind Mom owned. Belts crisscrossed over her chest.

"Is that supposed to be Pippi Longstocking?" I asked.

"This," Mrs. Hidalgo said, looking down at her arm, "is la Pippi."

"She looks like Pippi Longstocking, but not."

"When I was a kid, I was so obsessed with the Pippi Longstocking books that one year I decided to dress up as her for Halloween. I had the red wig and the mismatched socks and too-big shoes." Mrs. Hidalgo smiled, remembering her costume. "My mami made a patchwork dress even though she had no idea who Pippi Longstocking was. I even painted some freckles on my nose. I went all out."

"I've read those books," I said. "Cool costume idea."

"I thought so too," Mrs. Hidalgo said. "Until one of my friends laughed at me."

"Why?" I asked.

"She thought it was funny because Pippi is white and, well, obviously I'm not."

"But it was Halloween," I said. "The point of dressing up is that you can be anyone."

"Right?" Mrs. Hidalgo said. "I was nine, and it never dawned on me that I couldn't be Pippi, or anyone else for that matter. Not just on Halloween but whenever."

Mrs. Hidalgo carefully placed the powdered cookies into a storage container.

"Anyway, I drew this character when I was in college," she said. "It's Pippi with a Mexican twist. To remind me that I shouldn't let others decide who I can be."

"I like it," I said. "Does it help? Remind you, I mean?"

"Believe it or not, it does."

"That's really cool," I said, rolling the last of the polvorones.

"Well, m'ija, you have earned your cookies," Mrs. Hidalgo said. "Thank you for helping."

She wiped her hands on her apron and placed a few cookies onto a plate. "Share these with the band, okay? I'll be right down."

"Thanks," I said. "This was fun."

I took the cookies and headed to the basement, ready to start our first official band practice.

✂✂✂

"About time," Joe said as I came down the stairs. "Benny could've learned how to play the bass five times by now."

"Relax, I've got cookies," I said. "And your mom."

I set the plate down on the floor. Benny immediately pounced.

"These cookies taste . . . interesting." Ellie said, biting into one and studying it closely.

"If you aren't going to eat it, gimme," Benny said.

He snatched what was left of the cookie out of Ellie's hand. Ellie tried to take it back.

"Yo, stop it!" Joe said. "You fools are gonna break something in here."

"Sorry," Benny said. He and Ellie tried to clean up the cookie crumbs that had scattered.

When Joe's mom got to the basement, we officially started band practice. My job was to rewrite some of the lyrics to "Blitzkrieg Bop" and get rid of "objectionable content," as Mrs. Hidalgo had suggested. So I turned it into "Back to School Bop." This was a performance at school, after all. But I ended up mostly watching while Mrs. Hidalgo went from Ellie to Benny to Joe, helping each one with their parts. She showed them chords, where to move their hands, which part of the drums to hit and when. She was like a cool, good-smelling punk rock music teacher. I felt jealous that Joe had her as a mom, and watching them together made me miss Dad even more.

Joe and Benny played until their fingers started to blister. Ellie really seemed to understand what it meant to set the rhythm. It was almost like she discovered a talent she never knew she had. It made sense to me. She seemed like the kind of kid who was determined to do well at everything she tried.

The afternoon flew by, and when I finally looked at my phone, I saw that it was already after five.

"I gotta head out," Benny said. "Thanks for the help, Mrs. H."

"Anytime, Benny," Mrs. Hidalgo replied. "It's good to see you hanging out with Joe again. You used to be so close."

"Yeah, this was fun," Benny said, and bumped fists with Joe.

"We need to practice every day until the audition," I said. "Cool?"

Benny nodded and held out his fists to me and Ellie, and we bumped them too.

"We definitely need practice," Ellie said, following Benny out. "In case none of you noticed."

"Oh, we noticed," Joe said. He flailed his arms in an exaggerated air drumming motion. "See ya, Sheila E."

"Who's Sheila E?" Ellie asked.

"Only one of the greatest drummers ever," Mrs. Hidalgo said.

Ellie gave her a thumbs-up and grinned.

"I should head out too," I said, walking over to the crates of records.

"Be very careful with those," Joe said. He looked over at Mrs. Hidalgo, who was wrapping up a guitar cord, and whispered menacingly, "Or she'll kill you."

"I know how to handle records," I said. Flipping through the albums made me think of being at Spins & Needles. "I grew up in a record store."

"How sad for you." Joe made a face like he was about to cry.

"Be nice, José," Mrs. Hidalgo said in a warning tone. "Malú, I want to hear more about that later. But right now I want you to listen to something. Could you pull The Brat out of there, please?"

I moved my fingers through the *B*s to find the album. Sandwiched alphabetically after Bad Brains and before Best Coast was Lola Beltrán, the wailing lady with the spider-leg eyelashes. It was weird how she seemed to be everywhere. I still hadn't listened to the CD I'd borrowed from Señora Oralia.

I kept flipping until I spotted The Brat. There was only

one record. I recognized the cover from the wall at Calaca. The band photo had an eighties-punk look, all black and white on a red-and-orange background. The band's name was printed at the top in a funky font that included a backward *R*. At the bottom was the title of the album, *Attitudes*, written in white script that was visible against the black of the men's shirts. I pulled out the record and handed it to Mrs. Hidalgo.

She slipped the record out of its cardboard sleeve and placed it on the record player, then carefully lowered the needle onto the vinyl. I heard the familiar popping and crackling, my favorite sound in the whole world, and then the first song started.

It began with a reggae rhythm on guitar, those bouncy, staccato sounds that made me think of being at the beach. Then came the drums, heavy on the cymbals. And finally, a woman's voice that was like the hot chocolate Mom made in the winter, thick and warm and strong. The song went from its reggae intro to poppy punk. I couldn't resist moving to the beat. Okay, so maybe punks *did* dance.

"This is amazing," I said. "Who is she?"

I picked up the album cover and studied the photo of the woman whose voice sang out from the speakers.

"That's Teresa Covarrubias," Mrs. Hidalgo said. "The Brat was a Los Angeles band in the early eighties."

"This is so rad," I said.

"And they're Chicanos, Mexican Americans," Mrs. Hidalgo said. "Like us."

Like us. I repeated the words in my head. The next song came on. It was another fast pop-punk song with a reggae beat.

"I'm going to leave you two to your musical nerd fest," Joe said. "Later, María Luisa."

"Walk her home, Joe," Mrs. Hidalgo said. "Please."

"Do I have to?" Joe whined.

"I'll make you a mix sometime, Malú," Mrs. Hidalgo said, ignoring Joe. "You should know all punk has to offer, not just the standards. And you should know your people's influence on the genre. It's part of your history."

"Thanks, Mrs. H," I said, and followed Joe upstairs, still hearing the music in my head and Mrs. Hidalgo saying "like us." She must not have known that I'm a coconut who doesn't even eat cilantro.

"Your mom's great," I said to Joe as we walked back to my building. "You don't know how good you have it."

"She's all right," he said. "A little weird, but . . ."

"I haven't even told my mom about the band."

"Seriously?" Joe asked. "Why not?"

"She wouldn't like it," I said. "Anyway, she doesn't really have to know. As long as I do well in school and don't complain about being here, she's happy."

"If you say so," Joe said, sounding unconvinced.

"Practice at your place tomorrow, right?" I asked.

"Yeah," Joe said. "Tomorrow and forever, from the looks of it."

I thought about Mrs. Hidalgo saying that it was important to know my history. Mom had said the same thing when she was telling me about Posada. But the history Mom was talking about was totally different than the history Mrs. Hidalgo was talking about. Wasn't it?

Chapter 19

"Is that what you're wearing?"

Mom was like a scratched record with that question. She eyed the blue-and-green-plaid Catholic school jumper I wore. I'd found it on one of my thrift store adventures with Dad. Today I'd paired it with a white Spins & Needles Records T-shirt, blue striped tube socks, and my sequined Chucks. It was my punk Dorothy look.

"You're going to need something comfortable, something you can move in."

"You mean like this?" I asked. I jumped up and down and jogged in place, lifting my knees as high as I could.

Mom sighed. "Don't you think it's time you started acting and dressing like una señorita?"

"I'm wearing a dress," I said, and gave her a curtsy. "That's señorita-like."

Her look told me my outfit was not what she had in mind.

Even though Mom said it was "very rude," I put my headphones on for the train ride. She could drag me to this thing, but I didn't have to talk to her.

The dance school was in a huge warehouse-type building that also housed other businesses. The door had the words RAMIREZ DANCE STUDIO stenciled in big gold letters. Below it, in smaller letters, it read TEACHING MEXICAN FOLKLORIC DANCE SINCE 1998. Mom opened the door, and we were greeted by the sound of heels banging against the wooden floor.

Selena and a boy a little older than us stopped dancing. They were the only other people there besides Selena's mom. Señora Ramirez smiled big when she saw us. She turned off the music that was still playing and walked over.

"Magaly y María Luisa." She gave us both a hug. "I'm so glad you came. This is my son, Gael, and you know Selena." The two walked over, clopping the whole way like a couple of horses.

"Selena, get María Luisa a pair of shoes," Señora Ramirez said. "This is going to be fun."

For who?

"Sí, Mami," Selena said. "Come on, *María Luisa*."

"Shoes?" I asked, looking at Mom.

"Those won't do at all," Señora Ramirez said, pointing to my sneakers. "You need something with a hard heel to make some noise." She stomped her own shiny black shoes against the floor, and Mom gave a startled laugh.

"I don't think we're going to have anything to match that outfit," Selena said as we walked to a wall of cubbies full of shoes that reminded me of a bowling alley. "What size?"

"Very funny," I said. The cubbies were filled with the kinds of shoes I would never voluntarily wear. They had buckles and heels and wouldn't go well with cutoffs.

Selena handed me a pair of scuffed brown shoes in my size and walked back to where our moms waited. I changed into the shoes and clip-clopped to a case full of ribbons, sashes, certificates, trophies, and plaques. Some of them were awarded to Ramirez Dance Studio, but many were in Selena's or Gael's name. There were also photos of Ramirez dancers, most of them featuring Selena and her mom.

"Wow," Mom said. "She's really good, huh?"

Señora Ramirez beamed and nodded. "She and her brother have been dancing since they were little," she said. "Gael, come here. Why don't you two show them your dance for the Mexican Independence Day parade? We have a float that features our dancers every year."

Selena rolled her eyes. She looked annoyed as she turned to join her brother. But by the time she got into formation, she'd replaced her annoyed look with a big smile, her eyes crinkling at the corners.

When the music started, it sounded like tiny bells and jumping string instruments. I watched as Selena and her brother stomped back and forth and side to side. Selena lifted and bowed and waved her skirt so fast, it was dizzying. All the while she kept a smile on her face. Joe was right about the cucaracha killing. No bug that had the misfortune of finding itself under their shoes was coming out alive.

Out of the corner of my eye I could see Mom sway in place, smiling, like she wanted to jump in and dance too. Maybe she was thinking about what it would be like to have a daughter like Selena.

When the music stopped and the dance ended, Mom burst into applause. She nudged me with her elbow, and I clapped my hands a few times.

"Amazing," Mom said. "That was beautiful." If the look on her face was an emoji, it would be the smiley face with hearts for eyes.

Selena and her brother said thank you at the same time. Gael changed into his sneakers, said good-bye, and made a quick exit. The lucky dog.

"Well, let's show you some basic steps, ¿sí?" Señora Ramirez asked. "Selena, work with la Señora Morales, and I'll see if I can help María Luisa find a little rhythm."

Selena cackled like the Wicked Witch of the West. "Good luck with that, Mami," she said, leading Mom by the arm.

"A good teacher is encouraging, Selena," her mom said, taking my hand. She stomped out a beat, and I tried to follow, but my feet felt like they were weighed down by big Frankenstein shoes.

"Just loosen up," Señora Ramirez advised, shimmying

and waving her arms around like she was blowing in the wind. "Look, your mom has got it."

I looked over at Mom, who was laughing as she sashayed and stomped like it was the happiest day of her life. Meanwhile, I felt like the Tin Man, who'd been left out in the rain to rust, in need of some serious oil for his joints. I tried to remember the feeling I had at punk shows when the music just took over, and I felt free to move without being judged. This wasn't a punk show, though, and I felt ridiculous. So for the next hour I did what Dad had advised, and I just tried. But when Señora Ramirez went left, I went right. It seemed that no matter how much I tried to keep up with her, I couldn't. How did Selena do this?

"That was one of the most fun things I've ever done," Mom said when dance class was over. Her face was flushed, and strands of hair had come loose from her bun.

"You did great," Señora Ramirez said. "You too, María Luisa." She patted me on the shoulder in a consoling manner.

"Yeah, right," I mumbled.

"Our next session starts in two weeks if you'd like to sign up," Señora Ramirez said.

"Oh, I do," Mom said with a nod. I gave her a look of terror.

"Let me get you a brochure so you can see what we offer," Señora Ramirez said. "You can sign up online or just do it when you come in for the first class."

She walked toward the office, Selena following close behind.

"Mom, I'm not doing a whole session," I whispered urgently.

"Don't worry," Mom said. "I'm not going to force you to do it. I'm glad you at least tried."

"Good," I said, feeling like I was finally able to breathe. "I'm going to get my shoes." I couldn't wait to get out of there and meet the band for practice.

I walked back to the cubbies and sat down on a chair next to the office to put my sneakers back on as quickly as possible. If I didn't hurry, Mom might change her mind about signing me up for classes. From where I sat, I could hear Selena and her mom talk inside the office.

"What is this? Is it like the Riverdance?" Señora Ramirez asked.

"It's Irish dancing, Mom," Selena said.

"But you're not Irish. Why do you want to do Irish dancing?"

"It looks kind of cool," Selena said. "It's kind of like . . . like Irish huapango."

Señora Ramirez laughed. "That's the silliest thing I've heard. You don't have time for that, Selena."

"I promise it won't get in the way of my dancing here," Selena pleaded.

"I've already said no," Señora Ramirez said, sounding agitated. "Besides, you know this time of year is busy with Independence Day, el Día de los Muertos, las Posadas. We have too many obligations already."

"But, Mami—"

"No. Now come on," Señora Ramirez said, cutting her off. "They're waiting for us."

"Yes, Mami," Selena said.

I leaned low over my knee, pretending not to notice as they came out of the office. Selena balled up a piece of paper and threw it into the trash on the way to meet Mom. When Señora Ramirez started going over the brochure with Mom, I stuck my hand into the trash can and pulled out the paper Selena had thrown away. Once I smoothed it out, I could see it was a flyer for an Irish dance class at a neighborhood rec center. I quickly stuffed the paper into my pocket before joining Mom, who was at the door saying good-bye to Señora Ramirez.

"Are you sure that's your mom?" Selena asked, checking that the moms were out of earshot. "She can move, but you looked like a rag doll." She let out her Wicked Witch cackle.

I had actually started to feel a little bad for Selena after hearing Señora Ramirez shoot her down about the Irish dance lessons. But she made it really hard to sympathize with her.

"You're right," I said. "I could use a little spring in my step. Maybe a little *Irish* spring."

Selena looked at me like she was trying to see inside my head.

"Let's go," Mom called from the doorway.

"See you at school," I said, and gave Selena a smirk.

At first I felt pretty good about not letting Selena get the best of me, even though my Irish spring joke was kind of corny. But then I started to think about how her mom not letting her dance wasn't so different from my sneaking around with the band, afraid Mom wouldn't let me do it if she knew. I understood wanting something badly and feeling disappointed, even if I didn't get why she would want to go from one stomping dance to another. It was kind of like how in *The Outsiders*, Ponyboy and Cherry Valance are from completely different worlds, but they understand each other, at least in some ways. I tried to convince myself that punks don't feel guilty about giving mean people a taste of their own medicine, but by the time we got home, I felt even crummier about my joke.

Chapter 20

When the day of the talent show auditions arrived, I felt like we were as ready as we could be. We'd practiced every day, sometimes with Mrs. Hidalgo's help, and had watched a bunch of videos of the Ramones performing. I worked on my singing in the shower until Mom said she didn't know what she was going to do if she heard "that song" one more time. We knew we wouldn't sound perfect, but we'd have time to really work on the song after we got into the talent show.

Despite all our work, everything seemed to go wrong on that Thursday afternoon as we stood in front of Principal Rivera, Mr. Jackson, and Mrs. Larson, the music teacher. When we were setting up, Joe realized he'd left the cord to his guitar in his locker and had to run back to find it, which cut into the time we'd been given. Ellie counted us down, but all three of them managed to start playing their instruments at different times, so we had to start over. Worst of all, when it was time for me to sing, I opened my mouth, but nothing came out. My tongue felt like it had been glued to the roof of my mouth, and as much as I tried, it wouldn't unstick. When it finally did, I sounded like I was croaking out the lyrics. At least the ones I could remember. But croaking seemed to work great with the grating, mismatched sounds that came from the instruments behind me.

Halfway through the song, it felt like we were finally in sync. My face and ears burned. My stomach was still in a knot, and all I could do was clutch the microphone, but at least I wasn't croaking anymore. When we finished, Mr. Jackson and Mrs. Larson looked at each other, then at Principal Rivera, who jotted something down.

"Thank you for coming," Principal Rivera said with a smile. "We'll post the participants on the announcements board tomorrow."

We gathered our instruments, minus the drum set we'd borrowed from the band room, and left the auditorium. Outside, there were a few kids, including Selena, waiting their turn.

"I thought that went okay," Joe said.

"You're kidding, right?" I wanted to cry, partly from the relief of being done, but also because I knew we didn't sound anything like I imagined we would.

"Besides," Joe said. "The auditions are just a formality. Everyone gets into the talent show."

"What's the point of auditioning, then?" Benny asked.

"They just make you audition to, like, prescreen you," Joe said. "To check that what you do is, you know, *appropriate*."

I felt a little better after hearing that. But before I went to sleep that night, I made sure my worry dolls were under my pillow. We just needed more time, and we'd be ready to rock the talent show.

Chapter 21

The first thing I did when I got to school the next morning was check the announcements board where the talent show roster would be posted. I read name after name, scanning nervously for the Co-Co's. But we weren't on the list. What about what Joe had said? Didn't everyone get to perform? I knew we'd messed up, but I thought we'd get a chance to really prepare after the auditions. Except it looked like we wouldn't get that chance after all.

Mr. Jackson's office was nearby, so I walked over, part of me hoping he wouldn't be there. His door was open a crack. I knocked before poking my head in. He sat at his desk, eating oatmeal, the instant kind you mix with boiling water and eat out of a cardboard cup.

"Hi, Mr. Jackson," I said, rubbing the toe of one shoe

nervously over the other. "I have a question about the talent show, and I thought I'd ask you since you were at the auditions yesterday."

"Come on in." Mr. Jackson spun around in his chair to face me. He had a little bit of oatmeal on his beard. "You're . . . let me think. I know this."

I waited for him to remember my name while he chewed on a spoonful of oatmeal.

"María Luisa," he finally said with a self-satisfied smile.

"Malú," I corrected.

"Yes, so what's up, Malú?"

"Well, um, do you know why my band didn't get picked for the show?" I asked.

Mr. Jackson swiveled back and forth. He cleared his throat and rubbed his hand over his beard, finally wiping off the oatmeal. Then he gave me an apologetic smile.

"Yeah, the Co-Co's," he said. "Right on. You guys were pretty rockin'."

"So why aren't we on the list?" I asked.

"Well, as you probably know, this year marks the school's thirtieth anniversary. We're celebrating José Guadalupe Posada, and Principal Rivera wants the talent show to have an anniversary vibe to it," he said.

"What does that mean?"

"She wants to feature more traditional acts."

"Traditional how?" I asked.

"Well, we've got some singers, a violin player, a kid who does these cool lasso tricks. Have you seen him?"

I shook my head.

“He’s awesome,” Mr. Jackson said. “And one student is doing a folkloric dance, that type of thing. Acts Posada might enjoy if he was alive.”

“But there was nothing on the flyer that said we couldn’t play any song in any way,” I said. “Was there?”

“Hmm,” Mr. Jackson said, moving some papers around on his desk until he found the green flyer. He read over it, taking a bite of watery oatmeal. “You’re right. It says thirtieth anniversary, school appropriate, but nothing about specific types of acts.”

“I even rewrote some of the lyrics to the song so it would be okay for school,” I said.

“You guys were fun to watch,” Mr. Jackson said. “But I think Principal Rivera wants it to be family friendly, maybe a little . . . quieter than the Co-Co’s. I’m sorry.”

He had a sincere look on his face, but that didn’t make me feel any better.

“It’s okay,” I said. “Thanks.”

I left Mr. Jackson to finish his oatmeal. As I headed to first period, my ears burned with anger at the unfairness of it all. I couldn’t believe we’d been shut out of the talent show for being too loud.

✂✂✂

Ellie and Joe had already claimed a table when I walked into the library. We’d planned to meet up at the end of lunch to talk about the talent show.

"Please don't get any food on that book, Joe," Mr. Baca called from the circulation desk.

"Got it, Mr. B," Joe said, trying to brush bread crumbs off the pages of the book open in front of him so that Mr. Baca wouldn't see. "Did you guys know that the Maya thought crossed eyes were attractive?" He crossed his eyes and looked from me to Ellie with a straight face. "What do you think? Were they right?"

Ellie laughed and shook her head.

"Ugh, that does not feel good," Joe said, rubbing his eyes. "But who am I to argue with the Maya?"

"You are so weird," I said. "Where's Benny?"

"I'm coming, I'm coming," Benny said as the door to the library closed behind him. He put down his trumpet case and bag next to our table. "So, what happened?"

"Yeah, what did Mr. Jackson say?" Ellie asked. She had a puzzled look on her face. "Why weren't we picked?"

I shared with them what Mr. Jackson had told me that morning about Principal Rivera's plan for the Fall Fiesta talent show.

"And it's totally unfair," I said. "Because none of that was in the flyer, right?"

"But why would Principal Rivera do that?" Ellie asked.

"Duh," Joe said, frowning. "Because she hates punk music."

"Principal Rivera just made up an excuse to keep us out," I said.

"How does she even know Posada wouldn't like punk

music?" Benny asked. "How would any of us know that?"

I nodded. He had a point.

"You know what this is?" Joe asked. "This is—"

"Discrimination," Ellie finished for him.

"That's right," Joe said, pounding the table with his fist.

"But what can we do?" Benny asked. "She's already decided we aren't playing in the talent show. Which stinks because if I'd known this was going to happen, I would've just played with my band friends. They're in the show."

"We could start a petition," Ellie said. "Demand to be included."

"I don't know," I said. "That might work for some things, but I don't think it will work for this."

Joe, Ellie, and Benny looked at each other.

"Excuse me, but did I just hear you quit, punk rock girl?" Ellie asked. Her brow furrowed, and she stared at me intently.

"Yeah, we put a lot of time into this," Joe added.

"Again, what are we going to do?" Benny asked.

"I'll tell you what you're going to do right now." Mr. Baca came around the circulation desk and walked over. "You're going to head to class. Lunch is almost over, and I have a group coming in soon."

"Well?" Ellie whispered as we left the library. "What *are* we going to do, Malú?"

I had no idea. And I couldn't figure out what made me angrier: that Principal Rivera had basically discriminated against us because we played loud music that wasn't "traditional" enough or that Selena made it and we didn't.

✂✂✂

That night when I called Dad, the first thing he asked about was the talent show audition.

"It went really well," I said. "And we're going to play, too." I wasn't sure why I blurted out a lie, but I wanted to kick myself after the words came out of my mouth.

"That's fantastic! What'd Mom say?"

"Well, I haven't exactly told Mom about it."

"Lú, you have to tell her," Dad said.

"Of course," I said. "I will."

"Soon? Because if you don't . . ."

"Yeah, Dad, soon."

"Good," he said. "I'm really glad you've made friends. Some of my best friends are people I've played music with."

I thought about Joe and Benny and Ellie. I hadn't really thought about them as anything other than bandmates, but I guessed they *were* friends. Or at least the closest thing I had to friends. Although now that we weren't in the talent show, would we still hang out together?

"See, it's a good thing you had those worry dolls with you, right?"

"Totally, Dad," I said. "I guess they really work."

When we hung up, I sat down at my desk to work on a zine. The Lola Beltrán CD that Señora Oralia had loaned me caught my eye, sitting on top of a stack of library books. I opened the plastic case and slipped the disc into my computer. The first song started all mournful trumpets and violins. I lay back on my bed and wondered how many worries my little dolls could handle now that I had to add "lying to Dad."

When the CD finished playing, I searched online for videos of Lola performing. Her long, thin fingers, covered in rings, moved in dramatic gestures. Everything about her was big. Her hair, her jewelry, her voice. She was a pretty spectacular performer, just like the punk singers I loved. Just like I wanted to be too, if I ever got the chance.

Chapter 22

Señora Oralia's door was open a crack, and the smell of something delicious filled the hallway. Mom knocked, and we waited as footsteps shuffled toward the door.

"Vengan, muchachas," she said, grabbing us each by an arm. "We've been waiting for you."

She pulled us inside with a grip that was pretty strong for an old lady's.

"I made chilaquiles," she said. "I think you're going to like them."

"I *love* chilaquiles," Mom said.

Señora Oralia had invited us to Sunday dinner with her family. Joe, Mrs. Hidalgo, and Mr. Hidalgo, who looked like an older Joe with a mustache, were in the kitchen when we arrived. We greeted everyone, and Mom placed the bowl of bean and corn salad she'd made on the counter, which was already covered with enough food to feed more than six people.

"You want a pop?" Joe asked, holding out two bottles of bright red Jarritos.

"Pop?" I asked, taking one. "Don't you mean soda?"

"Maybe where you're from, dude."

I took a swig of the soda that tasted like fizzy strawberry candy.

"I hope the chilaquiles aren't too picosos," Señora Oralia said as we sat down to eat. "I like them spicy."

"Mamá, you know you're not supposed to eat spicy food," Mrs. Hidalgo said.

"Ay, look at this one talking to me like she's the mother," Señora Oralia said, and laughed. "What's a little spice now and then, right?"

"That's right, Bueli," Joe said, dishing up a spatula full of chilaquiles onto his plate.

"Don't encourage her, Joe," Mrs. Hidalgo warned. "What about you, Malú? Do you like spicy food?"

I felt like I was in the hot seat, no pun intended. But before I could answer, Mom jumped in.

"I'm afraid Malú didn't inherit the Mexican taste buds."

Everyone laughed except for me.

"Don't worry," Mr. Hidalgo said, rubbing his stomach. "You aren't the only one who can't handle spicy food."

I rolled my eyes at Mom and shoved a forkful of chilaquiles into my mouth to prove her wrong, immediately regretting it. I could feel my tongue slowly begin to throb as the heat of the peppers crawled over it like an army of tiny fire ants.

"Toma leche," Señora Oralia said, noticing my discomfort. "Milk helps with the spiciness."

"Too hot for you, huh, María Luisa?" Joe laughed. He didn't seem to have a problem with it. He had already devoured one serving and was going in for seconds. I stuck with Mom's salad, which was not spicy and was cilantro-free, and the plain enchiladas Mrs. Hidalgo brought.

After dinner Mr. Hidalgo made coffee, and Señora Oralia brought out a yummy-looking cake.

"I am so full," Mom said as Mrs. Hidalgo set out plates. "I don't know if I can eat another bite."

"You have to try at least a small slice," Mrs. Hidalgo said. "I need guinea pigs for this cake. It's a vegan tres leches."

"Be-gan? ¿Y qué es eso?" Señora Oralia asked Mrs. Hidalgo.

"It's an oxymoron," Mr. Hidalgo said, and laughed.

"*Vegan,*" Mrs. Hidalgo repeated. "That means it has no milk, no dairy."

"Oh boy," Joe whispered to me. "Here we go."

"¿Un postre de tres leches . . . sin leche?" Señora Oralia finally asked.

She shook her head and laughed. No, she guffawed. I remembered that word from a vocabulary list last year.

Señora Oralia's laugh was loud and boisterous from deep in her belly like it had been stored there, waiting for this specific moment. It was definitely a guffaw.

I had to admit, a vegan tres leches cake did sound a little bizarre, since I knew that tres leches means "three milks," and vegan means no dairy or animal products of any kind.

"That sounds interesting," Mom said. "But why vegan?"

"Believe it or not, we have a lot of people who come into the coffee shop who are looking for vegan alternatives, especially for baked goods," Mrs. Hidalgo said. "Even Mexicans, Mamá." She gave Señora Oralia a surprised look that was clearly exaggerated.

"Not these Mexicans, right, Bueli?" Joe asked, putting his arm around Señora Oralia. "We like our milk and eggs and butter."

"Ana always has to be different," Señora Oralia said. "Look different. Eat different. Think different."

I glanced at Mrs. Hidalgo, who was slicing the cake. She had a look on her face that I knew well, a look that said she'd heard this a million times.

"Tell me about it," Mom said, pointing her thumb in my direction. "This one is allergic to anything that she thinks is too 'normal.' Just like her dad."

"Jeez," I said. "We're right here." I looked at Mrs. Hidalgo, and she smiled and winked. It felt good to have someone who could be part of my "we." Especially someone like Mrs. Hidalgo.

"Bueli, tell them the story about when Mom came home with her first tattoo," Joe said.

"Ah sí," Señora Oralia said, waving her hands. "It's a miracle I didn't have a heart attack."

"You're so dramatic," Mrs. Hidalgo said, shaking her head.

"Mom said Bueli fainted and bumped her head and they had to take her to the hospital," Joe said.

"Really?" I asked. I couldn't believe it. Señora Oralia didn't seem like the kind of lady who would freak out over tattoos. Or over anything, really. I still remembered the purple nail polish she'd worn when I first met her.

"Pobrecita," Mrs. Hidalgo said. She reached over to pat Señora Oralia's shoulder. "She wouldn't talk to me for weeks. Remember, Mamá? For an entire month she'd leave me these little notes. It was ridiculous."

"My head hurt for days," Señora Oralia said. "And only part of it was because of the fall!" She looked at Mrs. Hidalgo with a twinkle in her eye. "Ana was always up to something. Tell them about when I had to pick you up at the police station."

"This sounds like an interesting story," Mom said.

"My mom, the lawbreaker," Joe said, and laughed.

"It was no big deal," Mrs. Hidalgo said as she distributed slices of cake.

"What happened?" I asked. I couldn't imagine Mrs. Hidalgo getting into trouble. What could she have possibly done?

"My high school had a pretty strict dress code for the homecoming dance. We couldn't wear sneakers, and our outfits had to be at least semiformal, so the boys had to wear jackets and ties," Mrs. Hidalgo said. "A group of us thought it was unfair."

"Unfair how?" Mom asked, slicing a bite of cake with her fork.

"Well, it discriminated against kids who couldn't afford to buy ties or jackets if they didn't already have them," Mrs. Hidalgo said. "Plus, some of us wanted to wear sneakers with our dresses."

"Estos muchachos had their own dance where they weren't supposed to be," Señora Oralia said, giving Mrs. Hidalgo a stern look like she'd just gotten the call from the police right at that moment and not years ago.

"Bueli's *still* mad," Joe said.

"We asked the administration to reconsider the dress code and be a little more lenient," Mrs. Hidalgo went on, ignoring Señora Oralia and Joe. "But they wouldn't. So we organized an anti–homecoming dance in protest."

"That's so rad," I said, glancing at Mom.

"You could come dressed as you pleased, fancy formal wear not required," Mrs. Hidalgo said with a nod. "And instead of an entrance fee, we asked for a donation, either money or food, for a local homeless shelter."

"So where do the police come into the story?" Mom asked. I could tell she wanted me to know that calls from the police were not okay.

Mrs. Hidalgo explained that they needed a space for their dance. They decided to use an empty garage that was owned by one kid's uncle. The only problem was that he never asked for permission, so when neighbors heard music and saw kids going in and out, they called the police.

"And you got caught?" I asked.

"We were trespassing on private property, so the police came. They called our parents and cut our dance short," Mrs. Hidalgo said.

"Were you arrested?" I asked.

"No. Contrary to what my mom said, we *weren't* taken to the police station." She shot Señora Oralia a stern look.

"Same thing," Señora Oralia said with a shrug. "The police called me to come get my delinquent daughter."

"We should have asked to use the garage, but kids make mistakes," Mrs. Hidalgo said.

"I can imagine how worried you were when you got a call from the police," Mom said to Señora Oralia, ignoring the fact that Mrs. Hidalgo had done the coolest thing ever.

"Pues, sí," she said. "I think she's in one place and she's somewhere else, making trouble."

"Not making trouble," Mrs. Hidalgo said. "I'm still glad that we stood up for what we believed was right."

"Psssh, she hasn't changed one bit," Señora Oralia said. But she didn't sound angry. It was more like she found the stories funny now.

"How can she be mad?" Mrs. Hidalgo asked, taking a bite of her cake. "The apple doesn't fall far from the tree, right, Mamá?"

"How did you ever get through it?" Mom asked, glancing at me. "Having a . . . contrarian daughter?"

"We did not always agree with each other," Señora Oralia said. "But I always told her to stand up for what she believes in, what comes from here." Señora Oralia put a fist to her heart.

"Even if it means getting arrested?" Joe asked.

Everyone laughed.

"It sounds like you have a pretty good relationship now," Mom said, looking from Señora Oralia to Mrs. Hidalgo.

"She still thinks I'm cuckoo," Mrs. Hidalgo said. "But she tries to understand who I am, and that we're all different in our own ways, right, Mamá?"

Señora Oralia reached over and stroked Mrs. Hidalgo's pink streak of hair.

"You're right, Ana," Mom said, surprising me. "I hadn't really thought about it, but I guess I was a contrarian too."

"You?" I asked.

"Yes, me," Mom said. "I left home to go to college. That was something no one in my family had ever done, but I felt like I needed to see more, find my place, you know?"

"And how did that go over with your family?" Mrs. Hidalgo asked.

Mom laughed. "Well, my parents were always supportive, but I think they would have preferred to be supportive from a closer distance," Mom said. "It was hard to leave them. I think it was just scary for everyone. Something different and unfamiliar. And it's still hard all these years later to be so far away from each other, but—"

"It's gotten easier?" Mr. Hidalgo asked.

"In some ways." Mom nodded. "Easier, but not easy."

Mom looked at me and smiled, and for a moment I thought maybe she actually understood.

"Ay, you American teenagers," Señora Oralia said. "Too much free time. In my day, you would be too busy working. No time for dancing or funny hair colors."

"And we'd be walking twelve miles to school in the desert too, right?" Joe's dad asked.

"School? ¿Qué school? You would be working, m'ijo."

We all laughed again.

"This has been so much fun," Mom said, and nudged me. "Gracias por todo, Señora."

"Thank you," I said. "I mean, muchas gracias." The Spanish words felt like they were stuck in my teeth. Whenever that happens, I get more self-conscious.

"You don't like to speak Spanish," Señora Oralia said. It was not so much a question as a declarative statement.

I shrugged, once again in the spotlight.

"She just doesn't speak it often, so she's not used to it," Mom said.

"It's good to have two languages," Señora Oralia said. "You know how I learned English? Listening to the Beatles."

"Really?" Mom asked.

"Sí, señora. I could not speak a word of English, but I

worked for a family who had a teenager. We would listen to records together. I was singing 'Twist and Shout' and didn't even know what any of it meant."

Señora Oralia let out another hearty guffaw and shook her head as if she couldn't believe what she was telling us.

"I used to be able to do the Twist, too—mira," she said as she started to move in her chair.

I tried to imagine a young Señora Oralia dancing to the Beatles, but I could only picture her the way she looked now—doing the Twist in the unicorn housedress she'd worn the first day we met her, fuzzy slippers on her feet. I smiled, thinking about it.

"Don't lose your language," Señora Oralia said, like words were something that might end up under the bed with mismatched socks and dust bunnies.

After dessert, I sat on Señora Oralia's flowery couch while Joe flipped through channels on the oldest television set I'd ever seen. It looked like a piece of furniture, the screen encased in wood and surrounded by little fake drawers.

I kept thinking about Mrs. Hidalgo and her anti-homecoming dance idea. How did she ever come up with such a great way to make a point? And wasn't she afraid of getting into trouble? She must have really believed in what she was doing to take that risk. At that moment she seemed like the bravest person I knew.

And then, like the Scarecrow who suddenly got a brain, a lightbulb went on. I jumped up from the couch, which must have startled Joe, because he dropped the rabbit ear antenna he was fiddling with.

"Band meeting at Calaca tomorrow after school," I said. "I'll tell Ellie. You let Benny know."

"But we didn't make the list," he said.

"It doesn't matter," I said with a smile. "The Co-Co's are just getting started."

Chapter 23

The next afternoon we sat around a table at Calaca, and I told the band my idea.

"So you want us to crash the Fall Fiesta talent show?" Ellie asked, like I'd just made the most scandalous announcement ever.

"No, we're not crashing it," I said. "We're throwing an anti–Fall Fiesta talent show instead."

"I like the way you think, dude," Joe said, picking concha frosting crumbs from my plate.

"Where are we going to do this anti-talent show?" Benny asked.

"That's why we're meeting," I said. "To work out the details. I can't think of everything myself, you know?"

"Excuuuse us," Joe said.

"This sounds really risky," Benny said.

"Look, the talent show is inside the school, in the auditorium, but Fall Fiesta is outside," Joe said. "We could just set up and play outside somewhere."

"Good idea," I said. "I can't imagine Principal Rivera's going to let us have our anti-talent show in the school anyway."

"Wait, won't we get into trouble for doing this?" Ellie asked. "*That* would not look good on a college application."

"Okay, Miss Fight-the-Power-One-Petition-at-a-Time," I said. "I know you care about students' rights. But sometimes petitions won't cut it. We're doing this for a good cause." I needed to convince myself too.

"And that cause is . . . ?" Ellie asked.

"There was nothing on the audition flyer about the talent show disqualifying certain types of acts, right?" I asked. "Principal Rivera handpicked the kids that fit her picture of what this thirtieth anniversary celebration should look like. Us? Our loud punk band? Not part of that picture."

"Big deal," Benny said, shrugging.

"It is a big deal," I said. "I mean, Mr. Jackson didn't say we were excluded because we made mistakes. She kept us out on purpose. Because she doesn't like that we're loud and not 'traditional' or 'family friendly.' Whatever that means."

"I'm with María Luisa on this," Joe said. "That's anti-weirdo discrimination."

He and Benny laughed.

"A lot of people in history *have* taken risks to make

social and political statements. . . ." Ellie added. "Count me in."

"We're a punk band, right?" I asked. "And punk means standing up for what you believe in. Just like Joe's mom. And like Poly Styrene, who wore plastic bags to protest consumer culture, and Joe Strummer, who wrote songs against war and oppression, and—"

By now I was out of my chair, pacing by our table.

"Okay, relax. I get it," Benny said. "I can't believe I'm agreeing to this."

"Besides, I bet we aren't the only kids who wanted to perform at the talent show but got left out because Principal Rivera didn't like what they did," I said.

"Well, can we at least call it something else?" Ellie asked. "Anti-talent show sounds so . . . negative."

"We could just call it the Alterna-Fiesta talent show instead," Joe said.

"That sounds cool," I said. "Joe, you think your mom would help us again?" I asked hopefully. "She did inspire the idea after all."

"Are you kidding me?" He had a get-serious expression on his face. "You know she'll eat this up like it's some vegan flan."

We all cracked up because we knew Joe was right. If anyone could help us pull this off, it was Mrs. Hidalgo. And she'd really understand why we wanted to do this.

A punkier version of a song I'd heard before started to play over the coffee shop's speakers.

"Y'all know this is my favorite song," Joe said. He

started to sing along and bob his head for a few seconds.

"'La bamba'?" Benny said. "For real?"

"I'm old-school like that," Joe said.

"Maybe we can do a punk version of an old Mexican song," I said. "Like this song that's playing."

After the words came out, I waited for them to laugh.

"I don't know," Ellie said. "If we're going to cover a song, it should be something that rocks, right?"

"Yeah," Benny said. "We don't want the kids to feel like they're hanging with their abuelas."

"Principal Rivera wants traditional and family friendly, right?" I asked. "So let's give it to her. But our way."

"I like it," Joe said. "Now you're thinking, María Luisa."

The song ended, and a female voice I now recognized as Lola Beltrán came on.

"I'll think of a song," I said, but I already had an idea. "Be ready to get to work tomorrow."

When I got home, I kicked off my shoes and grabbed my laptop. I plugged in my headphones, popped in Señora Oralia's Lola Beltrán CD, and waited for the music to start. Which old ranchera song could we turn into a cool punk rock song? "Paloma negra"? "Cucurrucucú paloma"? Lola B sure did like pigeons.

In "Soy infeliz," Lola B's deep, strong voice sang of love that wasn't reciprocated. Most of the songs were heavy, sad love songs that made you feel like you were drowning in tears. I didn't know anything about being in love, so none of them felt like the right song.

Then I heard one I recognized. I had a memory of

Mom singing along to it while she made breakfast on a lazy weekend morning. The tune was lighter and happier than the others. It was the opposite of a sad love song. The lyrics spoke of how singing could make hearts rejoice. I listened to the song over and over as I tried to imagine it louder and faster and with me singing it. I picked up the CD case and looked at the list of track titles. It was a song called "Cielito lindo."

Chapter 24

"I hate this thing," I said, yanking at the lock.

By the time I'd spun the dial left and right and left again for the third time, I decided that the combination lock was my sworn enemy.

"Step aside, tonta," Joe said, moving in on my locker. "What's your combination?"

"I'm not telling you my combination," I said, even though I knew my chances of seeing my history book were fading.

"Suit yourself," he said.

I tried my combination one more time and, unsuccessful, let the lock drop back against the locker with a loud clang.

"You giving up on this yet?" Joe asked.

"Fine, you try," I said. I dug out the slip of paper with my combo on it and handed it to him.

I watched as he turned the dial left, right, left, then pulled. The lock clicked and opened. He turned to me, a satisfied look on his face.

"Well, aren't you special?"

"A thank-you will do," Joe said. "Hey, did you think of a song?"

"I did," I said, grabbing my history book from my locker and stuffing it into my backpack.

"And?"

"I'll tell you at practice when we're all together," I said.

"You're gonna make me wait? Dude!"

Something flew across the hallway and landed at our feet. It was a candy necklace. Or what was left of it. There were a few candy beads hanging from the sad-looking elastic band.

"Score!" Selena said as she and a guy from her candy crew walked up. Joe slapped the guy's hand and fist-bumped, then stretched the necklace between his fingers and pulled it back like a slingshot, aiming it at Selena.

"¿Qué pasa, lovebirds?" she asked, holding her bag up to shield herself from the candy necklace. "That means . . ."

"I know what that means," I said, cutting her off. "Not funny."

"I couldn't be sure, María Luisa," she said. "I know you have trouble with your Spanish sometimes."

I slammed my locker door shut and snapped the lock closed.

"That's too bad you didn't make it into the talent show," she said.

"Yeah, too bad," Joe said. I gave him a look so he would zip his lips.

"See you later," I said to Joe, ignoring Selena and her friend. I hooked my arms through the straps of my backpack. I wanted to get out of there before Joe spilled the beans about our plan.

"Wait," Selena said. "Don't you need to kiss good-bye or something?"

I felt my ears burn as I walked away.

That afternoon, I had bigger things to worry about than Selena. Like how to get ready for our talent show while avoiding Mom. She suddenly had a lot of thoughts about my daily visits to Joe's after school.

"You two sure are spending a lot of time together," Mom had said that morning when I told her I was going to Joe's later.

"We're working on a school project," I had said defensively. "I thought you wanted me to make friends and be happy here."

"Pues, sí. I'm glad you aren't holed up in your room all the time."

Heading into Joe's basement, I felt like I'd slipped past Mom's curiosity and questions one more time. But I knew each time could be the last.

Joe, Benny, and Ellie sat in a half circle in the basement, looking both excited and nervous.

"So? What's your great idea?" Joe asked.

"You guys promise not to laugh?"

"We can't promise anything," Joe said. Benny fiddled with his bass, and Ellie pretended to take notes to avoid eye contact with me.

"This." I placed the Lola B CD on the floor in the middle of the circle.

"What are we going to do with that?" Joe asked.

"We're going to do a punk version of one of these songs," I said. "'Cielito lindo.'"

"Are you telling us you want to sing a punked-up version of a Lola Beltrán song?" Benny asked, like maybe his hearing had failed him.

"Yeah." I nodded, but my brain started to panic. What seemed like a great idea earlier suddenly felt like a sure disaster.

Joe stared at the cover, the big bouffant, the chandelier earrings, the pointy nails. Those long fingers. It felt like the seconds were dragging.

"Never mind," I said, grabbing the CD. "We can come up with something else."

"No, wait. I can see it," Joe said. "But maybe the band should take a vote."

"Yeah, okay," I said.

"Are there any objections?" Joe asked, and looked to each of us.

"Not from me," Benny said. "This is more my style anyway."

"Yeah, who knew your trumpet-playing skills would come in handy, right, Ben?" Joe said, and laughed.

"Can I listen to it first?" Ellie asked.

Joe queued up the song, and we all watched Ellie as she closed her eyes and listened. Everyone at Posada Middle took Spanish, but Ellie wasn't a native speaker, so I wondered how much she understood. Ellie kept a stone face the whole time, and it was hard to read her.

"I caught some of the words," she said when the song finished. "But what's it about?"

Ellie listened intently while Joe translated the lyrics as best as he could. Then we all watched as a big grin spread across her face.

"This is the song," she said. "It's beautiful and powerful, and I dare Principal Rivera to object. Let's do it."

"That was easy," Joe said. "And now you can prove to Selena once and for all that you aren't a coconut."

I kicked him in the shin.

"Ow. Come on, I was just joking," he said, rubbing his leg. "But seriously, and don't take this the wrong way. Can you even sing in Spanish?"

"Don't listen to him, Malú," Ellie said. "You're super determined. You convinced me, someone who couldn't even play an instrument, to join the band. I'm pretty sure you can do anything."

"Thanks, Ellie," I said, and gave her a smile.

"You believed that I could play drums," Ellie continued. "Well, I think you can sing in Spanish."

Could I sing in Spanish? Joe's question played in my mind on repeat as I walked home. It was really cool the way Ellie had come to my defense, but I wasn't so sure I believed in me as much as she believed in me. Having to sing in Spanish was kind of a big detail to overlook. It was one thing to say "hola" and another thing to sing an entire song. I thought about what Señora Oralia had said about singing along to Beatles songs even though she couldn't speak English. If she could do that, maybe I could sing in Spanish.

Yes, I told myself as I arranged the worry dolls under my pillow that night. I could sing in Spanish. But as I looked into their little dotted faces, doubt crept over me again like a cold fog. Couldn't I?

MUSIC...

29
EL TAMBOR
MUSIC
is
MAGIC
Cool
DYNAMIC
smart
INSPIRATION
MY
MUSE
!

6 REASONS WHY I ♥

1

It's like a language. Sometimes I have a feeling but words aren't enough. Like when you feel like the tinkling wind chimes at the beginning of a song or like the squeaking sound when fingers move across guitar strings. Do you know those feelings too?

2
Like a good
book, a good song
takes me places.
My mind gets lost
in the sounds
and words.
It helps me
feel connected
to people. Especially
to my dad.
3
4
When I sing
I feel . . .

STRONG
and
SURE
Like I am in
control of something.
Like I am creating
something.

5
I don't know if I can even sing EN ESPAÑOL, but when I heard . . .
("pretty little sky")
CIELITO LINDO
I knew it was my song to sing. Sure, it's a little lovey and sappy, but it expresses how music makes me feel most of all:
HAPPY!!

The lyrics say: Ay ay ay ay, sing and don't cry, because hearts become happy by singing. Except in Spanish, of course. Singing and listening to music makes my heart happy and hopeful.

6

Lately music has made me feel more connected to the Mexican part of me. I don't know if it's from listening to Lola B so much or from learning about Mexican punk from Mrs. H, but it's kind of . . . cool.

IS
MY
JAM
M

Chapter 25

"Of course you can sing in Spanish," Mrs. Hidalgo said. We were in the Hidalgos' basement the next afternoon, and Joe had filled her in on our plan. As expected, she was more than willing to help.

"I don't know," I said nervously. "Maybe this isn't the best idea after all."

"Save it," Ellie said. She twirled a drumstick in her hand with an attitude that said she wasn't in the mood to accept self-deprecating comments.

"You heard the story my mother told. She could *sing* in English before she could speak English. And Ritchie Valens couldn't speak Spanish when he sang 'La Bamba,'" Mrs. Hidalgo said. "Besides, it's an easy song to learn, and since you already know Spanish, it won't be a problem.

You just have to memorize the lyrics and believe you can do it. Right, Joe?"

"You got this, dude," Joe said with a thumbs-up.

"Maybe your mom can help you with the singing too," Mrs. Hidalgo suggested.

"Her mom doesn't even know she's in a band," Joe said, and laughed.

"What?" Mrs. Hidalgo looked surprised. "Really? Why?"

I glared at Joe for opening his big mouth. "I don't think she'd like that I'm spending my time on a band instead of doing something more productive." I made air quotes to indicate that "productive" was one of Mom's words. "Plus, punk bands aren't the kind of thing señoritas are into."

"Says who?" Mrs. Hidalgo asked, her hands on her hips. "I think you should give your mom a chance, and you definitely need to tell her. I can't help you behind her back. I believe in your right to rock, but I also abide by the Mom Code."

"What does she think you're doing after school anyway?" Benny asked.

"Chess club?" Ellie offered.

"Something like that," I said. "I tell her I'm at Calaca, doing homework, or helping Mr. Baca in the library. As long as she thinks I'm getting involved and happy here, she's totally fine."

"Well, you *are* getting involved with school," Benny said.

"I think your mom would be happy to know that you're doing something you really enjoy with friends," Mrs. Hidalgo said.

"What's wrong with being in a band?" Ellie asked. "It's not like you're out robbing banks."

"You guys don't know SuperMexican," I said. Benny, Joe, and Ellie laughed. "It's not just about being in a band. And I don't want to talk about it anymore, okay? I'll tell her soon. Can we just get to work?"

Mrs. Hidalgo put a hand on my shoulder and leaned in close. "Sooner than later will be best," she said. "Let me know if you want some help."

"Thanks," I said. "I will." But I still wasn't convinced that I ever had to let Mom know about the Co-Co's.

"By the way, I've played this song before," Benny said, pulling his trumpet out of its case. He inhaled, put the trumpet to his lips, and played "Cielito lindo."

"Wow," I said when he finished. "You're really good."

Benny shrugged, looking embarrassed.

"You ready to sing, María Luisa?" Joe asked.

"Now?"

"Yes, now," Joe said. "Or are you waiting for a written invitation?"

"Why don't we start working on the music," Mrs. Hidalgo said, "and give Malú time to get the lyrics down, all right?"

"Yeah," I said, fanning my sweaty armpits and waiting for the ground to swallow me up. "That sounds good."

I got the group to talk about talent show details before we wrapped up for the afternoon. I managed to go the whole practice without singing.

"We'll need a flyer," I said. "Something we can hand

out to kids who might be interested in performing or who want to see us."

"I'll draw something cool," Joe said. "Something funky, maybe with some Posada influences." He grinned conspiratorially. "And I bet Mr. Baca would let me use the copier in the library."

"Awesome," I said. "We're really doing this."

"You think you'll be ready to sing next time?" Benny asked.

I chewed on the inside of my lip and tried not to freak out at the thought of singing in Spanish.

"Earth to Malú," Joe said. "You're not gonna chicken out on us, are you?"

Joe started clucking and flapping his arms like a chicken until Ellie gave him a playful shove.

"She's not chickening out, right?" Ellie asked, and smiled.

"I'm *not* chickening out," I said. "I'll be ready."

Maybe if I said it enough times, it would be true.

Chapter 26

In the days that followed, I studied the lyrics to "Cielito lindo" and listened to Lola B on loop. I'd read the lyrics so many times, I could almost see them pass before my eyes like they were on a digital news ticker. Around and around they went. I read them before bed. I whisper-sang them in the bathroom as I got ready for school. In math class I slipped them inside my binder. And I sang them silently in my head during lunch while the band goofed around.

More than a week into practicing the song, the band finally played what sounded like "Cielito lindo."

"Once you have the song down, you can play around with the tempo," Mrs. Hidalgo said.

"Or it could just be chaos," Joe said. "It is punk rock, after all."

"Very funny," Mrs. Hidalgo said.

"What's the tempo?" I asked.

"Like 'tiempo' in Spanish," Benny said. "The timing."

"Right now it's a sweet slow dance," Mrs. Hidalgo said. "But you want to play it faster. Like it's a . . ."

"Frenzied mosh pit!" I said.

We all cracked up.

"Something like that," Mrs. Hidalgo said. "So, you ready to sing today?"

The stomachache I'd had on and off all day had come back. My palms were sweaty, and my cheeks were flushed. I knew I shouldn't feel nervous—it was just Ellie, Joe, and Benny—but I was. Very. I felt like the Cowardly Lion in need of courage.

"I think so," I said. "But you all have to promise not to laugh."

"Why would anyone laugh?" Mrs. Hidalgo asked, looking sternly at Joe.

"Come on, Malú," Ellie said. "You can do this."

"Okay," I said, nodding. "I'm ready."

Ellie counted down. Benny started his part on the trumpet. I opened my mouth to sing, but nothing came out.

"Sorry," I croaked. "Start again."

Ellie counted down again and Benny played, but all I could do was squeak out the first few lyrics.

"Loosen up those trenzas," Joe said. He reached over and tugged one of my braids.

I tried to swallow, but my mouth felt like a desert.

"Can I get some water?"

Mrs. Hidalgo went to the kitchen and came back a minute later with a glass of water that I instantly gulped down.

"Not so fast," Joe said, taking the glass out of my hand. "You're gonna get the hiccups."

"Closing your eyes might help," Mrs. Hidalgo said. "Imagine you're alone in your room. Or that you're singing in the shower."

I nodded.

"Here we go," Joe said. "For real this time."

I took a deep breath and waited for the clicks of Ellie's drumsticks. I closed my eyes and tried to imagine myself alone in the room, like Mrs. Hidalgo had suggested. And then, on cue, I sang like I'd been singing in my head and in whispers for days now.

I opened one eye. I was still in the basement. The band was still there, busy with their instruments. No one stared or laughed. So I kept singing. I'd studied the words so much by then that they traveled easily from my brain to my mouth. I *knew* this song, but it still felt like I was struggling to make the words feel like my own. When I finished singing I opened my eyes.

"Well?" I asked.

"That was actually . . . not bad," Joe said.

"Gee, thanks a lot."

"Don't listen to him," Ellie said. "You were great!"

"Beautiful," Mrs. Hidalgo said. Benny didn't say anything, but he gave me a thumbs-up.

"I have to admit, I was a little worried about your

Spanish," Joe said. "I thought it would sound funny. You being a coconut and all."

"Takes one to know one, right?" I asked.

"Seriously, though," he said. "You have a good voice, dude."

A wave of relief washed over me.

"Now we just have to kick it up a bit so it doesn't sound so sad," Ellie said.

"Good idea, Ell," I said.

"We should add some background vocals like in the song," Benny said.

"Yeah," I said. "Maybe we can sing the chorus together."

We went through the song a few more times. My body felt like a tightly wound coil, but it wasn't just nervousness anymore. It was excitement. Each time I sang, the words felt more natural coming out of my mouth. Like me and Spanish might belong together after all if we gave each other a chance.

Chapter 27

When October rolled in, the weather began to cool. And then the most amazing thing happened. Autumn! Everything turned fiery red and gold like in that Robert Frost poem in *The Outsiders*. I loved the sound of the leaves crunching under my shoes and the smell of wood burning. Mom and I took a trip to a farmers' market where I discovered that there are so many different types of apples and that my new favorite food was the apple cider doughnut. I wanted to bottle up all the smells and colors and the feeling of fall so they'd always be close. I wished I could iron it all between sheets of wax paper like I'd done with the bright red maple leaf I'd mailed to Dad. And the weird thing was that when I remembered we had another fall in Chicago, I didn't feel as unhappy as I thought I would.

October also meant that the Fall Fiesta was looming, and it was getting harder to find excuses for why I needed to stay after school or go to Joe's. I felt like Mom was giving me funny looks. Like maybe she knew I wasn't being 100 percent truthful.

"Joe isn't . . . your boyfriend, is he?" Mom asked one morning. She put down her newspaper and looked at me with raised eyebrows. Her smile told me she was joking, but I didn't find the joke funny at all.

"Hilarious, Mom," I said sarcastically. "Why are you being gross?"

"Why is that gross?" she asked. "He's a cute kid. And he's artsy just like you."

"Joe is *not* my boyfriend." I rolled my eyes.

"Besides," she said, "you're getting to be una señorita. I mean, you could stand to look more like one, but that's beside the point. Boys are going to be interested, and you might be interested too. . . ."

"I cannot believe we are talking about this," I said, cutting her off. I grabbed one of the million apples we'd brought back from our farmers' market trip and stomped off to my room to call Dad before going to Calaca to meet up with the band.

"But if he was, you would tell me, right?" Mom called after me.

I could hear her giggle at the so-not-funny joke. Okay, truth? Joe wasn't bad looking, but that wasn't the point. On the one hand, I felt relieved that she didn't seem to suspect anything about the band. On the other hand, she had totally creeped me out with her boyfriend talk.

When Dad answered, he was walking Martí. I could hear the jingle of the dog's tags in the background, and I thought of the path he usually took, wondering where they might be at the moment.

"Dad, do you think Martí remembers me?"

"Of course he does," Dad said.

"But what if dogs have terrible memories?" I asked.

"Lú, this dog has known you all his life," Dad said. "Believe me, he remembers you."

"Okay, I was starting to worry," I said. "We've been gone for more than a month already."

"Hard to believe," Dad said. "Thanksgiving will be here before you know it. Hey, before I forget: I have a surprise for you."

"You do? What is it?"

"I can't tell you yet."

"Ugh," I said. "You know I hate surprises."

"I know, but you're going to have to wait for this one."

"Dad, seriously," I said. "Just tell me, please."

"Sorry, kid. Can't," Dad said. "But I can guarantee you'll like it."

"You promise it won't be one of those bad surprises?" I asked. "Like moving to Chicago?"

"It won't be one of those bad surprises," Dad said. "Trust me. Speaking of surprises, have you told your mom about the band?"

"No," I said. I filled him in on practicing with Mrs. Hidalgo and that she'd even offered to help me talk to Mom.

"I can help you talk to Mom too," Dad said. "If that's what you need."

"I know you can, Dad," I said. "But you don't get it like Mrs. Hidalgo does."

I felt bad as soon as the words came out of my mouth. I realized it was the first time I'd ever thought there was something Dad just couldn't really help me with.

"Of course I get it," Dad said. "You're scared your mom will be angry."

"It's not just that," I explained. "It's different with Mrs. Hidalgo."

"Yeah?" Dad asked. "What's special about this magical Mrs. Hidalgo?"

I knew Dad was joking, but something in the sound of his voice told me his feelings were hurt. I tried to choose my words carefully.

"Well, she's like me. She's a girl. And she's Mexican. *And* she's into punk. So it's like she understands all this stuff about me—"

"That I don't," Dad finished for me.

"I'm sorry, Dad," I said.

There was silence. Then I heard Dad sigh. "It's okay. Nothing to be sorry about," he said.

"I'll tell Mom myself," I said. It was the only thing I could think of to make Dad feel like I wasn't picking Mrs. Hidalgo over him. I'd never wanted to end a conversation as much as I wanted to end this one.

"No worries, Lú," he said. But it didn't sound like he meant it, at least not all the way.

All of a sudden liking fall in Chicago and being in a band and having friends made me feel like a traitor. How could I miss home and be happy here, too? I wondered if Dad secretly felt like *I'd* forgotten all about *him*.

✂✂✂

When I walked into Calaca, Joe was at the counter, bent over a notebook. Ellie and Benny weren't there yet. I waved to Joe and found a table, where I pulled out my zine supplies.

"What's that?" Joe asked when he came over. He nudged his chin toward the zine I was working on.

"It's a zine," I said, closing the cover of my book over it.

"What's a zine? Can I see it?"

"Maybe when it's finished." I told him all about zines and how to make them.

"Sounds cool," he said. "Are there, like, comic zines?"

"Yeah, of course," I said.

"Maybe I'll make one too then," he said. "Been working on a story." He tapped his sketch pad.

"What's it about?"

"A family of Mexican vampires," he said, and hissed. "They gotta figure out how to keep a tan and avoid the sun at the same time. But it's, like, the 1800s, so there are no tanning beds. Chew on that."

"Like I said before, you're weird," I replied, and laughed.

"But get this: instead of garlic, you should make their weakness cilantro."

"Good idea," Joe said. "I'm using that." He flipped open his sketch pad and wrote something down.

"You want your usual?"

I nodded.

"One Cafe Olé and one concha coming up."

Joe picked up his sketch pad and headed back behind the counter.

Through the window, I could see Ellie climb out of a car and wave to a red-haired woman in the driver's seat. When she arrived at our table, she dropped her heavy backpack onto the floor.

"What's in there?" I asked. "A ton of bricks?"

"Close," Ellie said. "These are all the books I need for the essay and test I have this week."

"Was that your mom? The woman in the car?"

Ellie nodded. "Couldn't you tell?"

"Yeah," I said, and laughed. "Do you live nearby?"

"Not really," Ellie said. "But I've been at Posada since kindergarten. My parents applied because it has a curriculum that will prepare me to complete a high school IB program. Which will look—"

"Great on a college application," I finished for her.

"Exactly." Ellie grinned. "They also want me to be in a school where I can easily learn a second language. It's worth being an outsider to get a good education."

"You're not an outsider," I said. I realized I didn't know

much about Ellie outside of the band and her school interests.

"My mom says it builds character," Ellie said with a shrug. "That it's good to know what it feels like to not be the norm."

"Girl, that's harsh." Joe placed a plate of conchas in the middle of the table just as Benny came in and made a beeline for our table.

"What's harsh?" Benny asked, grabbing a concha.

"Forget it," Joe said. "Check this out." He sat down and flipped through his sketch pad until he found the page he was looking for. He held it out for us to see. "I'm thinking we should make T-shirts."

We all leaned in to get a better look. On the page was a drawing of four coconuts, real coconuts, wearing mariachi hats. Above the coconuts was the band's name written over an eighties-looking checkered pattern.

"This is awesome," I said.

"What about a motto or a mission statement on the back too?" Ellie said. "Something like—"

"Like 'Not Your Abuela's Ranchera,'" I said.

"How about 'Not Your Abuela's Music,'" said Joe. "In case we decide to branch out."

"Or 'Spreading Mexican Culture. Loudly,'" Ellie added.

We laughed.

"And we should give one to Principal Rivera after the show," Benny said.

We argued over colors, mission statements, and eco-friendly T-shirt vendors. Then we asked Mrs. Hidalgo if Calaca Coffee would want to sponsor the shirts. And for a little while I was able to forget about my conversation with Dad and about eventually having to tell Mom about the band. It was the happiest I'd felt since we moved to Chicago.

Chapter 28

"What do you think?" Joe asked. We were in the library after school, where I flipped through a book I'd pulled from the display shelf while he finished the flyer for our talent show.

"Looks great," I said. "Did you check with Mr. Baca about the copier?"

"Yeah, no problem," he said. "I'll make the copies now."

"Cool," I said. "We can hand them out on Monday. We should probably do it off school grounds, just in case. Maybe by the bus stop."

Joe nodded and looked over the flyer again.

"And no color paper," I added. "We don't want it to be too noticeable."

"Yes, your highness," Joe said, bowing dramatically. "Whatcha reading there?"

I closed the book and held it up for Joe. I'd pulled a book from Mr. Baca's display about José Guadalupe Posada, the guy our school is named after and who our school was celebrating at the Fall Fiesta.

"He was a pretty interesting guy," I said. "I think I'm going to check this out before Mr. Baca closes up. I'll come by Calaca this weekend to grab some flyers."

Later, as I shoved the book into my bag, I found the balled-up flyer Selena had thrown away at her mom's dance studio. I pulled it out. The deadline to register for the dance class had passed. I wondered if Selena was still upset about it. Was she mad at her mom for not letting her do it? I didn't know why I'd even kept the flyer. Or why, as much as Selena bugged me, I felt a little bit bad for her.

✂✂✂

On Monday morning the four of us met early to give out as many of the flyers as we could. We hung out near the bus stop, at the end of the curb, where we wouldn't be noticed by school staff patrolling. It's the same corner where there's a little market perfect for buying bottles of orange juice and roles de canela, cinnamon rolls packaged in bright pink wrappers featuring a white bear wearing a baker's hat.

"All done," Ellie said.

"I think that went well." Benny laughed, pointing to a kid throwing the flyer into a trash can.

"Great," I said.

"Hey, that's my hard work," Joe complained. "Whatever. I know at least a couple of kids who are interested."

"Really?" I asked.

"Yeah," he said. "Rivera gave them the ax because their entire comedy act consisted of fart and bathroom jokes."

The bell rang, and we headed to our homerooms.

Selena and I had a routine now that consisted of ignoring each other at first, making faces from across the aisle, and eventually trading smart-aleck remarks. So it was no surprise when she leaned toward me to say something.

"I know what you're up to, María Luisa," she whispered cryptically.

"What are you talking about?" I asked, trying not to sound nervous.

We had strategically planned our flyer distribution to not only avoid teachers and staff, but also to avoid Selena. I knew Selena always arrived at school just as the bell rang and would come in through the front door instead of around the back, where everyone was supposed to enter. We also hadn't put any of our names on the flyer. Just the date, time, location, and invitation for kids to participate.

"You know what I'm talking about," she said.

"No, I don't," I said, fiddling with the cap on my water bottle.

"I know about your talent show plan." She pulled a sheet of paper out of her folder and placed it on her desk where I could see it. It was the flyer Joe had made. Not a copy of the flyer, but the original he'd photocopied in the library.

"Where did you get that?" I asked, before I could stop myself.

"I found it in Mr. Baca's copier, right where you left it."

"All that candy-necklace sugar is affecting your brain," I said. She had no proof it was mine, after all. "I've never used Mr. Baca's copier."

"You didn't, but Joe did. Mr. Baca said Joe must've forgotten it when I found it in the copier," she went on. "I offered to return it to him."

She gave me a smug smile.

"So what?" I asked. "We aren't doing anything wrong."

"Then why are you being so sneaky?" she asked.

"Why do you care so much? Just give it to me."

"No way," she said, putting the paper back in her folder. "I'll hold on to it."

Selena turned to her friend, letting me know we were done talking. I imagined pouring my bottle of water on her and watching her melt, like the Wicked Witch of the West, until there was nothing but a pile of clothes and a candy necklace.

I spent the morning distracted, wondering what Selena planned to do with the flyer and then, just before lunch, I found out.

The PA in my science classroom crackled to life.

"Ms. Freedman, can you please send María Luisa to the office?"

The whole class looked up from their microscopes, where we were studying plant cells, and faced me.

"Go on," Ms. Freedman said. "Take your things."

When I walked into the front office, Mrs. Soto, the school secretary, looked up.

"María Luisa?"

I nodded. I didn't even bother correcting her, because I was so nervous.

"Principal Rivera would like to see you," she said. "Come on back. Her office is at the end of the hallway."

I walked through the little swinging door that separated the offices from the waiting area, and headed down the hall. I'd never been inside a principal's office. All the while I thought about how in *Ramona Quimby, Age 8,* Beezus told Ramona that she could remember the correct way to spell principal by remembering that the school principal was her "pal." Yeah right.

Principal Rivera was staring at her computer screen when I walked up to her door.

"María Luisa," she said when she noticed me. "Come in. Have a seat."

I sat down on one of the chairs in front of her super-neat desk. Notepads stacked to her right, a manila folder in front of her, and a calendar to her left. There was a fancy nameplate that read PRINCIPAL L. RIVERA right in front of me. I wondered what the *L* stood for.

"Is something wrong?" I asked, sitting on the edge of the chair.

"You tell me." Principal Rivera placed her hands on top of the manila folder and waited.

I stood up and did the fingertip test on my dress, hoping it was that.

"Your dress is fine," she said, and opened the folder. "María Luisa, it's come to my attention that you and your friends are planning to disrupt the Fall Fiesta."

"Disrupt the Fall Fiesta?" I asked. "That's not true."

I really was surprised to hear that. The plan was never to disrupt Fall Fiesta with our talent show. We just wanted to be part of it without being judged.

Principal Rivera opened the folder and slid a piece of paper toward me. I didn't even have to look at it to know what it was. It was the original flyer Joe had made.

"Can you explain this?"

I stared at the flyer and tried to think of what to say, but nothing that wasn't a flat-out lie or the entire angry and uncensored truth came to mind. So I didn't say anything.

"María Luisa, this is a warning. If you and your friends disrupt Fall Fiesta, there will be consequences."

She looked at my face, searching for my line of vision, but I just stared at the flyer.

"You've been doing very well here so far, but this won't be tolerated. Do you understand?"

I nodded.

"Good," she said, and glanced at the clock on the wall next to her. "Is this your lunch period?"

"Yes," I said.

"Mine too." She smiled as she pulled out a lunch bag from her drawer. "Go on to the cafeteria."

I got up and grabbed my bag.

"Fall Fiesta is a long-standing Posada tradition, and it's

a lot of fun," Principal Rivera said. "I hope you enjoy it, María Luisa."

Yeah, as long as my skirt was long enough and my talent show performance was traditional. As I walked toward the cafeteria, I felt angry at everyone: Joe for leaving the flyer in the copier, Selena for being such a busybody and giving the flyer to Principal Rivera, Principal Rivera for not letting us perform, or Mom for bringing me to this place.

Chapter 29

I let my tray smack hard against the lunch table before sitting down. Dad says if something is bothering me, I should just say it, but I was too angry to know what to say, and it felt good to let the tray hit the table.

"Whoa, easy there," Joe said.

I gave him the evil eye and chewed angrily on a sporkful of salad.

"You look mad," Benny said. "What's up?"

"I heard you got called into Principal Rivera's office," Ellie said, tearing her spork-and-napkin packet open.

"I did get called in to see her," I said. "And I am definitely mad."

"Are you going to tell us why or are you just going to take it out on that salad?" Benny asked, giving my salad a sympathetic look.

"Did you happen to notice you're missing something?" I asked Joe, putting down my spork.

Benny looked between us. "Should we leave?" he asked.

"What are you talking about, girl?" Joe asked, looking genuinely confused.

"Yeah, what's he missing?" Ellie asked.

"You left the original flyer in Mr. Baca's copier, dummy," I said.

"Aw, man, sorry." Joe gave me an apologetic grin before taking a sip of his chocolate milk. "I couldn't find it, but I thought it just got mixed in with the copies or something."

"Well, guess who found it," I said.

"Why don't you just say what you have to say?" Joe asked. "What happened?"

I told them the whole story then sat back with my arms crossed, scowling at Joe.

"So what? Principal Rivera knows," Joe said. "What's the problem?"

"Didn't you hear what I just said? There will be 'consequences' if we do this."

"Who knew you were such a quitter, María Luisa," Joe said, shaking his head.

"I'm not a quitter. *You* messed up the whole plan, *José*. How could you be so careless? If Principal Rivera thinks we're disrupting the Fall Fiesta, we could get detention forever. Or worse."

Joe's face started to get red. "Wow, María Luisa," he said. "You're the one who runs around talking about being punk. What now?"

"Well, you didn't have to talk to the principal," I said. "And your mom would probably support you if you got in trouble."

"I messed up," Joe said. "I said I was sorry."

"Well, sorry isn't going to fix this," I said.

"Maybe you should just tell your—" Ellie started before Joe cut her off.

"You know what? That's cool, 'cause I'm done with this band thing," Joe said. "*You* started this, *you* picked the song, *you* decided what we were all gonna do. I guess *you* get to call it quits."

Joe stood and picked up his tray.

"Later, Ellie. Later, Benny," he said, ignoring me.

"Wait," Ellie said. "What just happened here?"

"Yeah, is he for real?" Benny asked.

I couldn't answer because I didn't know what had just happened. I let a soggy piece of iceberg lettuce drop from my spork. The bell rang, and we gathered our trays.

"Can you believe him?" I asked, banging my tray on the side of the garbage can so hard, one of the lunch ladies glared at me.

"Malú, you were kind of hard on him," Ellie said. "Maybe if you talk to him, you two can figure it out."

"Yeah." Benny nodded. "Fall Fiesta is next weekend, and we've been working hard to get ready for this plan that *you* came up with, so let's do it."

"What do you want me to do?" I asked. "If Joe wants to quit, then I guess we are done."

"Just apologize, and let's move on," Ellie said.

"Me?" I couldn't believe Ellie. "He's the one who left the flyer for Selena to find."

"You heard him," Benny said. "It was an accident."

I wanted to get far away from Ellie and Benny, but they blocked my way, waiting for me to say something.

"I see projects to the end, Malú," Ellie said. She had an intense look on her face. "I even stopped working on my next petition to do this. You can't let this happen."

"Yeah, what about us?" Benny asked. "I passed up on a chance to play with band kids because you needed people for the Co-Co's."

"And what about all those flyers we gave out?" Ellie added. "There are other kids who were left out of the talent show who may be counting on the Alterna-Fiesta show."

I waited for them to move, completely annoyed. Finally Benny did, and I walked away. But I could barely see where I was going because my eyes were starting to well up with tears. Were the Co-Co's really done?

Chapter 30

It felt like someone had cracked open the Co-Co's and spilled all the coconut water out of them. Joe and I didn't speak to each other after our argument on Monday. With every day that passed, it got harder to say anything to him. Besides, he owed *me* an apology. It was his fault Principal Rivera had called me into her office. I started bringing something to eat from home and spending lunch in the library again to avoid the band—ex-band—in the cafeteria. I was back to where I was when I'd started at Posada. Friendless and eating alone.

"What's wrong with you?" Mom asked on Thursday afternoon. I was lying on my bed, headphones over my ears, listening to a song that reminded me of Dad and home. Not only were things over with the band, but since our last conversation, I felt like talking and texting with

Dad was awkward. Even though he kept reassuring me, I was afraid he really did feel like I was picking Mrs. Hidalgo's advice over his.

"Nothing's wrong," I said.

"You've been moping around all week. Are you sick?"

She put her hand to my forehead.

"I'm not sick, Mom," I said.

"Did you have an argument with Joe?" she asked. "I noticed you haven't visited him the last few days."

"It's nothing," I said. "I'm fine."

"Are you going to be okay to go to Fall Fiesta on Saturday?" she asked. "It's supposed to be fun. And I support anything that helps the school."

"No," I said. "I'm not going."

Mom sighed and shook her head a little, making the oval-shaped Guadalupe earrings she wore move. The little Guadalupes swung on their crescent moons back and forth, back and forth, like girls on playground swings.

"Okay, Malú, I'm not going to pry, but—"

"I thought you said you weren't going to pry."

"But," Mom continued, "I know moving away from Dad and everything you know and love, everything you listed in that zine you left in my bag, hasn't been easy."

"You read it?" I didn't think she'd even bothered.

"Of course I did," Mom said.

"So why did you bring me here anyway?" I asked.

"Malú, I loved your zine, but you knew it wasn't going to change anything, right?" Mom asked. "Look, I know that finding Calaca and becoming friends with Joe has helped you feel at least a little more comfortable here. I don't know what's going on between you two, but I hope you can work it out. It's been good to see you happy."

I pulled my pillow over my face and waited for her to leave. It was probably just as well we weren't doing the talent show. It was all a silly plan. A punk rock "Cielito lindo" and me singing in Spanish? We'd probably end up looking ridiculous.

"Hey, I need some coffee badly," she said. "Would you please go to Calaca with me?"

I hadn't been to Calaca all week. But what if Joe was there? Mrs. Hidalgo would surely be around, and I didn't think I could face her, either.

"I can't," I said.

"Let me know if you change your mind," Mom said. "I'm leaving soon."

I stayed behind my pillow until she left the room. The sun was shining in through the windows, the autumn light hitting the wall I'd decorated with pictures of bands. I'd discovered that the way the sun shines in the fall is exactly like writers describe it in books. I always thought it was something they made up, but it's true that even though it was starting to get cold, all the colors around me looked warmer and richer and made me feel like I was wrapped in a fuzzy blanket. I grabbed my book and headphones and went outside to sit on the porch.

Señora Oralia was camped out with her music and her crocheting supplies.

"¿Y esa cara?" Señora Oralia asked, looking up.

"Is there something on my face?" I wiped my mouth with my hand.

"Sí," she replied. "Tristeza. What makes you sad?"

I sat down on the swing and watched her hands move quickly as she worked her single needle and a ball of yarn into what looked like another toilet paper cover.

"Nothing," I said.

"Hmph," Señora Oralia grunted. "I didn't just fall off the cilantro truck."

I imagined a truck full of cilantro. I would jump off that thing, not wait to fall off.

"My Joe has been sad too," she said. "What's going on with you kids?"

"He has?" I asked. I'd seen Joe around school, but I didn't think he looked especially broken up.

"Is it love?" she asked with a twinkle in her eye. I felt my face turn red.

"No way," I said, a little louder than I'd planned.

"Mmmhmm," she said, and smiled.

"It's not," I said indignantly. "Our band broke up."

"Like the Beatles, ¿no?" Señora Oralia asked.

"It's not like the Beatles," I said, even though I had no idea why or how the Beatles had broken up. "I think I messed up."

"Bueno, and what do you do when you make a mess?" Señora Oralia asked.

"Clean it up?"

Señora Oralia didn't say anything. She just kept crocheting. The front door opened, and Mom came out. She greeted Señora Oralia.

"I'm leaving," she said to me. "Last chance to walk with your favorite mom."

Señora Oralia laughed, and I rolled my eyes.

"Is your plan to just never go to Calaca again?" she asked. "I know Mrs. Hidalgo would hate for that to happen."

I thought about the coffee and Mrs. Hidalgo's vegan treats and my favorite conchas. I didn't want to stay away from Calaca. I missed it. I missed Mrs. Hidalgo. And I missed Joe, too. So I got up, and we said good-bye to Señora Oralia.

"Bring me back un marranito," she called after us. "But not a be-gan one!"

Inside Calaca, the smell of coffee filled the air, and a band I recognized from our first practice played over the speakers. Mrs. Hidalgo was busy placing flowers on a table against a wall. She looked up when we walked in.

"Magaly and Malú," she greeted us, and waved us over. "Come here, I want to show you something."

"An ofrenda?" Mom asked as we walked over to the table. "Ay, Ana, it's beautiful."

"What is it?" I asked.

"An ofrenda is an offering," Mrs. Hidalgo said. "We've been doing this every year for el Día de los Muertos since we opened. Anyone can bring photos or items to honor loved ones who have died, and place them on this altar."

"It's a way to celebrate and remember," Mom said. "We

should bring a photo of Abuelo. What do you think?"

I nodded and looked at the smiling faces in the old, yellowed photos and the not-so-old photos that were set on the table. The surface was covered in overlapping rebozos of different colors. Bright marigolds looked like little suns sprouting from glass jars. White skulls had colorful sequin eyes and pretty designs on their faces.

"Those skulls are made of sugar," Mrs. Hidalgo said.

"Really?" My eyes widened. "Can you eat them?"

"Sure," Mom said. "Your dentist won't mind."

She and Mrs. Hidalgo laughed.

"It's great once people start leaving things because the table fills with all kinds of items. These items tell stories, and you get a sense of all the lives and interests of the departed and how much people still love and miss them," Mrs. Hidalgo said. She ran her fingers gently over a shiny harmonica and smiled. "This belonged to my papá. He used to sit outside after dinner and play it."

"It's lovely, Ana," Mom said.

"If you have something you want to bring for your abuelo, I would really love that."

"We definitely will," Mom said. "This is a great way to keep this tradition alive and to share it with the community."

"I'll leave some space for you, then," Mrs. Hidalgo said. "Now, why don't you two grab a seat, and I'll be over in a minute to take your order."

I started to follow Mom, but Mrs. Hidalgo stopped me with a hand on my arm.

"I know what happened, Malú, and I'm sorry to hear you and Joe aren't speaking," she said. "He's been down all week."

I didn't know what to say. Should I tell Mrs. Hidalgo that I was sad about the band too?

"He's in the back if you want to talk, okay?"

"I don't know," I said.

"You guys worked really hard. And the world needs the Co-Co's." She smiled like she meant it.

"Thanks, Mrs. Hidalgo," I said.

I wasn't in a hurry to sit with Mom, so I browsed the bookcase near Frida. "Cielito lindo" came on, and I listened to Lola B sing like I probably never would. I was sure Mrs. Hidalgo had played it just for me. A picture book about a bird called the quetzal caught my eye. The illustrations showed a little green fuzzy-headed creature. It looked like it had spiked hair—a little punk rock bird. Its long tail feathers were green and turquois, and a bright splash of red feathers covered its breast.

"What's that?"

I closed the book on my finger and turned around to find Joe.

"It's the resplendent quetzal," I said, shifting my weight from one foot to another. I was nervous and didn't know what to say, so I showed him the page.

"That bird is so not cute," Joe said. He rubbed the back of his neck. I could tell he was nervous too.

"It says here that the quetzal was sacred to the Aztec and Maya people," I said.

"Sacred, huh?" Joe repeated. "That's cool."

I took one last look at the little bird before closing the book and placing it back on the shelf.

"My mom told me you were here," Joe said.

"I'm here," I said. I looked down at my shoes, rubbing the tape off one with the sole of the other one.

"I'm sorry about the flyer," Joe said.

"It's okay," I said. "I'm sorry I got so mad."

"I should've been more careful." He shrugged.

"Yeah, well, it's done," I said. "And I guess it wasn't as big a deal as I made it."

"So what's up with the band?" Joe asked. "Are we really over?"

"I don't know," I said. "There hasn't been a band this week, that's for sure."

"We could still do this," Joe said. "It's not too late."

"But we haven't practiced in days," I said. "Besides, Principal Rivera knows about our plan."

"Well, does she really know our plan?" Joe asked. "All she saw was a flyer. Big deal. And we weren't going to set up inside the school, right? We could just start up after the talent show ends. That way we get more of an audience anyway."

"I guess you're right," I said.

"There's no way Rivera can accuse us of 'disrupting,'" Joe went on. "And if we do, it's for a good reason, right?"

I thought about it. I'd already accepted that we weren't a band anymore, but I really did want to do it. Even if it was risky.

"Come on," Joe said. "This was your idea. I mean, we could do it without you, but I sing like an alley cat."

"That's true," I said, and laughed.

"Besides," Joe went on. "We coconuts gotta stick together."

"Yeah, okay," I said, pretending he had twisted my arm. "Let's do it."

"Wait here," Joe said. "I have something for you."

He ran into the back room and returned a minute later, pulling something out of a bag and tossing it to me. I shook it out and held up a T-shirt.

"This is *the* raddest thing ever," I said.

The red T-shirt had the band's name and four coconuts wearing mariachi hats printed in black just like Joe had drawn in his sketch pad. On the back was the motto we had chosen: NOT YOUR ABUELA'S MUSIC.

"I can't believe you made these after everything that happened," I said.

"I made them over the weekend and was going to give them out at Monday's practice," Joe said. "But . . ."

"That never happened," I finished for him. I rolled up the shirt so Mom wouldn't see it.

"So then we're on for Saturday?" he asked.

"For sure," I said. "Let's get one last practice in tomorrow."

"Cool," Joe said. "What about Benny and Ellie?"

"I'll take care of that," I said. I just hoped they would still want to be part of the band too.

CALAVERA

El día de los muertos
is NOT Mexican
Halloween!

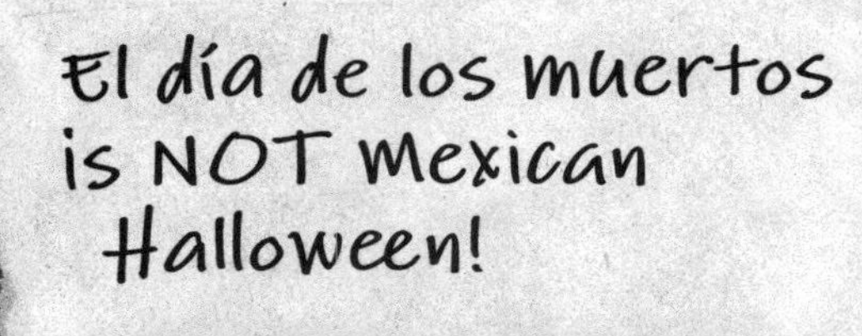

It's not about
being scared, wearing
costumes, or getting
candy.

It's about remembering
the people you love who
have died. And welcoming
them back!

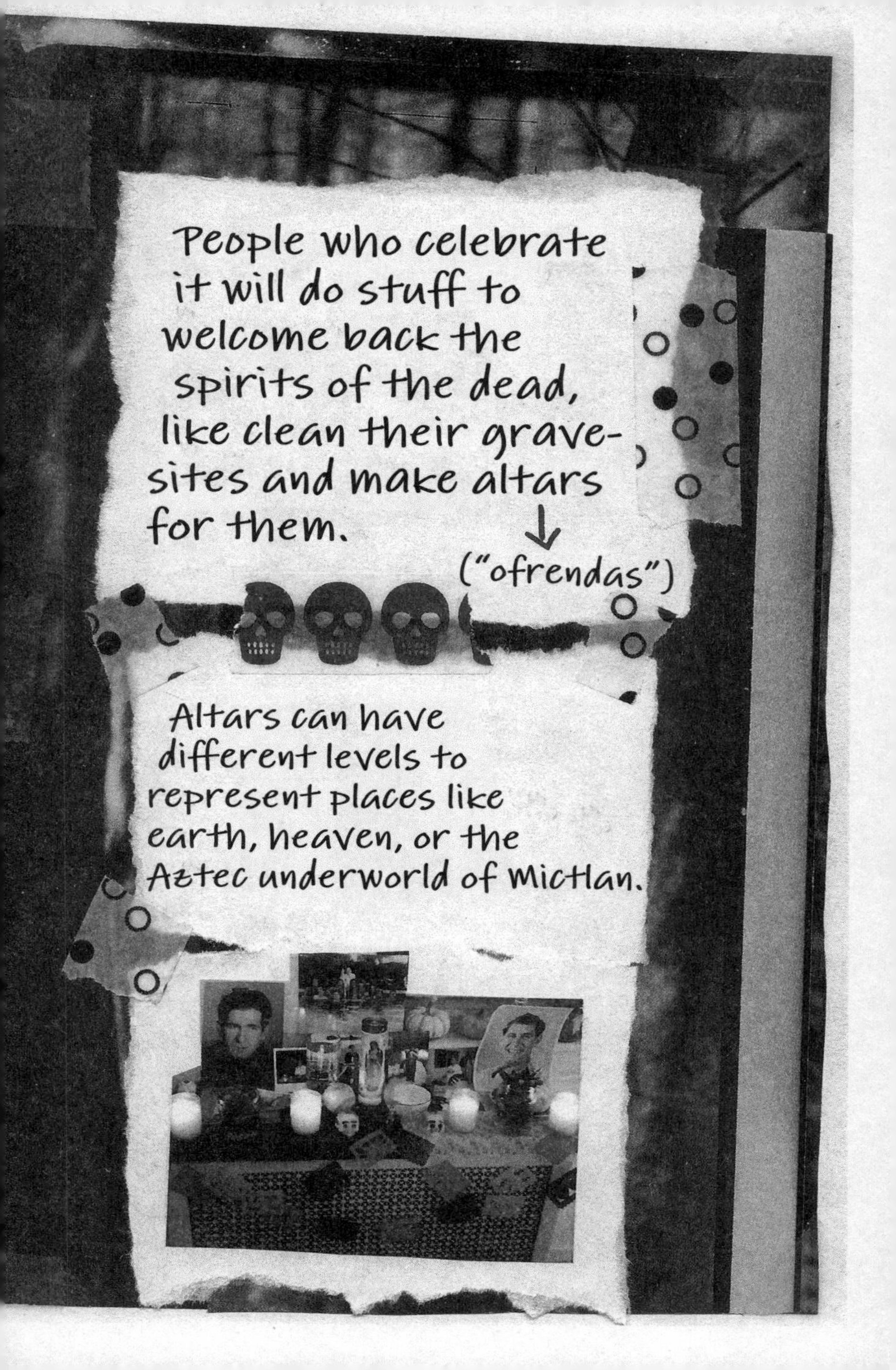
People who celebrate it will do stuff to welcome back the spirits of the dead, like clean their grave-sites and make altars for them.
("ofrendas")
Altars can have different levels to represent places like earth, heaven, or the Aztec underworld of Mictlan.

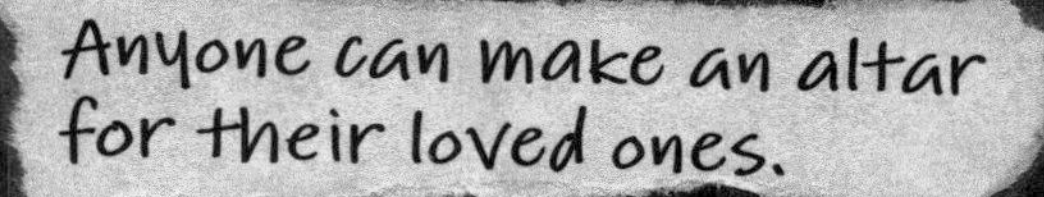

You just need a few things.

photos

favorite foods

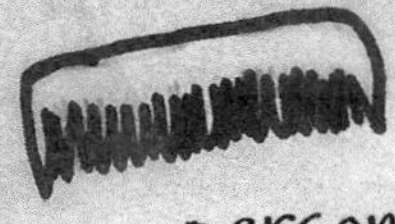

personal items

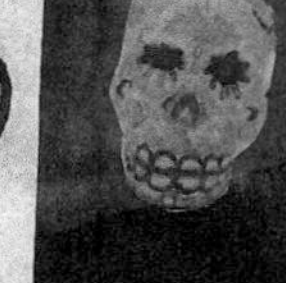

sugar skulls

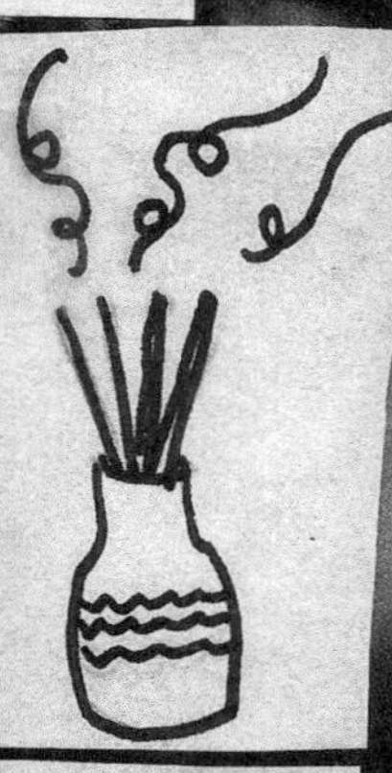

incense (copal)

But most important of all you need love and memories. Put your altar together and honor your loved ones on November 1 and November 2!

They weren't easy to find, but I am leaving a bag of Abuelo's favorite candy on the community altar at Calaca.

Orange Gummy Slices!

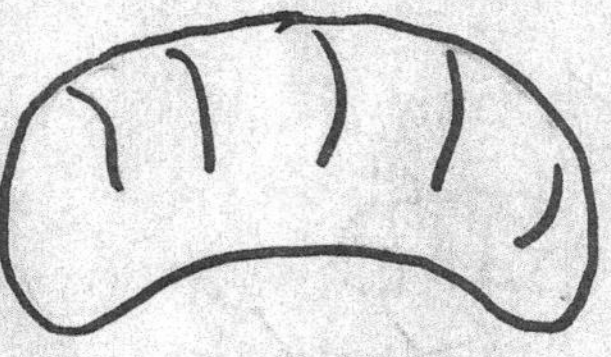

This is one of the most famous images you see around the Day of the Dead. Her name is La Catrina and she was created by . . .

José Guadalupe Posada

He is known today for his calaveras. (skulls) They look like people doing everyday things. They remind us that underneath our differences we are the same.

COOL

REMEMBER
M

Chapter 31

I sent a text message to everyone asking them to meet at our table in the cafeteria on Friday. And then I worried that no one would show up. I was so nervous that I stuffed my worry dolls into the pocket of my jeans to have them with me at school that day.

I decided to go to the cafeteria a few minutes late just in case no one came. Eating alone wasn't fun. Eating alone because you got stood up was worse. But when I peered in through the cafeteria window, I could see Ellie's red hair. She sat next to Benny who sat across from Joe. I skipped the lunch line and headed straight for the table.

"Look who's here," Joe said, dipping his spork into his mashed potatoes. "How's it going, María Luisa?"

Benny looked up and nodded. Ellie said hello but didn't smile.

"Can I join you?" I asked.

"You called the meeting," Benny said. Joe patted the seat next to him.

I sat down and took a deep breath. This was even worse than the nerves I felt when I sang. At least those were excited, happy nerves. These were the kind of nerves that made me feel like my insides were being squeezed.

"I need to meet with Mr. Jackson about organizing a canned food drive for the holidays," Ellie said. "So what's this about, Malú?" She had the same intense look as the last time we were together in the cafeteria.

"Okay," I said, wondering if they could hear my heart pounding. "I know you guys are angry with me. And I don't blame you. I just wanted to say that . . . I'm sorry."

"Sorry about what?" Joe asked, urging me on.

"I'm sorry I overreacted about Joe leaving the flyer in the copy machine," I said. "And I'm sorry I didn't fight to keep our band together."

"That's great, thanks," Ellie said, gathering her trash onto her tray and standing up. "I have to go. I'll see you guys."

"Wait," I said. "I'm not done."

I dug out a yellow business-size envelope from my bag. I'd spent the night working on a zine and had gotten to school early to see if Mr. Baca would let me make copies before homeroom. I pulled the three zines out of the envelope and handed them one each.

"What's this?" Benny asked, flipping through it.

"It's a zine I made about the band," I said. "I totally

understand if you guys don't want to do the talent show anymore, but if you still do, I would really like that."

In that moment, I felt like I was sitting behind an X-ray machine, and everything inside me was on display. My pounding heart, my scrunched-up stomach, all my hope, but mostly just a lot of fear that they wouldn't want to be part of the band anymore. I watched and waited as they each looked through the pages. Ellie closed her zine first. I held my breath, waiting for her to say something.

The zine was my version of *The Wizard of Oz*. Ellie was the brainy Scarecrow, Benny was the courageous Lion, and Joe was the Tin Man, all heart. I almost made Selena the Wicked Witch of the West, but decided to give that part to Principal Rivera. Mrs. Hidalgo was Glinda. And I was Dorothy, of course. We traveled down the yellow brick road together, our destination being the Alterna-Fiesta.

"This is really cool, Malú," she said. "I'm glad we're a band too. And I'll gladly be your Scarecrow."

"Does that mean you still want to see this thing to the end?" I asked.

Ellie came around the table and hugged me.

"You know that's the only way I roll," she said.

We both laughed. I gave her a big smile.

"Well, you already know I'm down, María Luisa," Joe said. "What about you, Benny?"

We all turned to Benny. He was the only one of us who was a real musician, and we needed him.

"Benny," I said. "I know you could've played with anyone at the Fall Fiesta talent show, but you picked our band. That means a lot to me, and I'm sorry I acted like it didn't."

"The band may be just something you're doing for fun," Benny said. "But I take music seriously. So, yeah, it was disappointing."

"It's important to me, too," I said, hoping he would see that I was being genuine. "Please say you'll play with us."

"Please?" Joe asked, batting his eyes at Benny.

"Pretty please?" Ellie chimed in.

Benny resisted, but a smile slowly formed on his face. "Fine," he said. "The courageous Lion can't let you knuckleheads go out there alone."

"Yeah!" I jumped out of my seat and did a little dance. "The Co-Co's are back, baby!"

One of the lunchroom monitors shot me the stink eye. I gave her a shy wave and slipped back into my chair.

"Practice today?" Benny asked. "We should get one more in since we've blown the whole week. The Co-Co's are never going to be a real band if we don't practice."

"Yes, maestro," Joe said.

"He's right," I said. "Meet at Joe's after school?"

"For sure," Ellie said. "But now I do really have to go. Mr. Jackson's waiting for me in the library."

"Can I come with you?" I asked. "I can help with the canned food drive."

"You don't have to," Ellie said, picking up her bag and tray. "I'm doing the band anyway. And I know canned food drives aren't exactly punk."

"Helping people is totally punk," I said, and grinned,

realizing that not only did I really want to help, but that it would be a chance to get to know Ellie better too.

"Well then, yeah," Ellie said. "I won't turn away help."

We said good-bye to the boys, but as we walked away, I thought of something.

"I'll meet you there," I said to Ellie. "I need to ask Joe something."

Joe was in the lunch line, grabbing another carton of chocolate milk. I passed the Candy Crew's table and hoped I wouldn't get stopped by Selena.

"What *is* that?" I heard Diana squeal. She peeked over Selena's shoulder at the screen of her phone. I caught a glimpse of the screen, where a girl with super-curly hair, really big like the hair on Señora Oralia's toilet paper dolls, danced. She wore a green dress with a round, flouncy skirt and white ankle socks, and as she stomped and kicked her heels, her curls bounced like each one had a coil inside.

"It's Irish dancing," Selena said, quickly turning off the phone so that the screen went black.

"Why are you watching that weirdo dancing?" Diana asked, and laughed. I could see Selena's face redden as she stood up and shoved the phone into the back pocket of her jeans.

I'd never seen Selena look embarrassed, so I did the only thing you do when you see something shocking: I stared. Selena noticed, and her eyes bugged at me.

"What?" she asked.

I looked away and quickened my pace.

"Thought you were going to collect cans," Joe said,

wiping off a chocolate milk mustache when I walked up.

"I am," I said. "But I need you to help me with something tomorrow morning. Early. Can you come over?"

He looked at me suspiciously.

"Am I going to regret it?"

"It's nothing bad," I said. "I promise."

"I'll be there, dude."

"Thanks," I said, relieved. This was definitely a job I couldn't do alone. It was nice to have a friend to count on.

Chapter 32

On Saturday morning I woke up before my alarm went off, and jumped out of bed like I had springs under my feet. I pulled on the outfit I'd picked out the night before: my Co-Co's T-shirt with the neck and sleeves cut off over a red tank top, turquoise pencil skirt over fluorescent-green leggings, and my silver Converse. I was rocking my quetzal colors for luck. To finish the look, I grabbed some black rubber bracelets to wear on my right arm.

In the kitchen, Mom stacked pancakes onto a plate.

"Blueberry-and-cashew pancakes?" I asked. "What's the occasion?"

"Why do I need a special occasion to make pancakes?" Mom asked.

"Because blueberry-and-cashew pancakes are usually

a special-occasion breakfast," I said, and sat down at the table.

"Well, happy weekend," Mom said, and placed a plate in front of me. "I thought we'd have a nice breakfast. You've been so down lately, and I wanted to cheer you up."

"Thanks, Mom," I said, still suspicious.

"Besides, it's good to change things up once in a while."

"Yeah, sure," I agreed, pouring maple syrup over my pancakes.

"You look nice today," Mom said.

"Are you okay, Mom?" I asked. "I'm worried about you."

"I'm great," she said. "Can't I tell you that you look nice?"

"Now you're really making me nervous."

"I like that shirt, by the way," she said.

"Oh, thanks. Just something Joe made," I said, shoveling a forkful of pancake into my mouth and hoping she wouldn't ask any follow-up questions.

I thought about that thing Mom sometimes says, something about a tangled web and lying. Could she see the guilt all over my face?

"So you two made up?" she asked, and winked.

"Please, Mom."

"Okay, okay," she said. "I'm gone. I have to go to my office today. Midterm grades are due, and I have a lot of essays to get through. I don't know if I'm even going to be able to make it to Fall Fiesta."

It had slipped my mind that Mom planned to attend Fall Fiesta. But this worked out perfectly. If she wasn't going to be able to make it, there was nothing to worry about.

"Thanks for the pancakes," I said.

She came up behind me and planted a kiss on my cheek. "Love you."

Something was up, but I didn't have time to wonder what it might be. I had bigger things to worry about. Joe would be coming over soon, and my stomach felt like the inside of a popcorn machine full of exploding kernels.

In the bathroom, I bent over the sink and splashed cold water on my face. When I came up, I caught my reflection in the mirror. Hair in two braids, just like always, but not for much longer. The buzzer rang, and I let Joe into the building.

"Dude," Joe said when I opened the door. "You should ask who it is. You never know when it's going to be el Cucuy coming to take you away in a big plastic garbage bag."

"I knew it was you," I said. "Even though you do look like el Cucuy." I laughed, and Joe swung his bag of supplies at me. Joe didn't really look like the boogeyman.

"You sure you want to do this?" Joe asked.

"You sure you know what you're doing?" I replied.

"Let the master show you how it's done," he said. "But first you're going to have to put on something you won't mind staining."

In my room I changed into an old T-shirt and cutoffs. I definitely didn't want to stain my stage outfit.

"Ready?"

"You aren't going to mess this up, are you?" I asked.

"Let's step into my office," Joe said as I led the way to the bathroom. "You're in good hands."

The whole process took a lot longer than I imagined it would, and the smell of chemicals irritated my eyes and nose. I was pretty sure hair bleach was not something a couple of kids like us should be messing with. But finally, Joe was ready to show me his work.

"Pretty cool if I do say so myself," he said, nodding his approval.

I turned to look at the left side of my head, then the right. "Let me see the back," I said.

Joe handed me a small mirror, and I held it up to see. He had cut off most of my hair. It was shorter than it had ever been, shaved close on both sides, with long bangs. The bleach Joe applied to my bangs left my hair a shade of yellow like the marigolds on Mrs. Hidalgo's altar. I'd decided to only dye my bangs, since I knew I'd have to color my hair again after the weekend or risk being in violation of the dress code. My heart pounded fast just thinking about the reaction Mom would have when she saw what I'd done.

"That's as blonde as we have time for," Joe said. "I hope the color looks okay."

"Thanks for doing this."

"No problem," Joe said. "If I never make it as an artist, I can always do hair."

"Can I ask you a question?"

"Sure," Joe said. "But I can't promise I'll answer it."

"Why'd you have your hair dyed blue on the first day of school?" I asked. "I mean, you aren't especially punky."

"I like the color blue. Why else?" Joe asked. "Besides,

there's no rule that says only punks can dye their hair, is there?"

"I guess not," I said. I looked him up and down. He was dressed in his usual Henry Huggins style, like a 1950s paperboy. Today he wore a striped T-shirt and rolled up jeans.

"Your problem is, you think punk is about the way someone looks," Joe said with a smirk. "Or the music someone listens to."

"Well, that's part of it," I said. "Sort of."

"Whatever you say, María Luisa," Joe said with a shrug. "You ready, punk?" He held up the container of hair dye.

"Yeah, keep working," I said. "We're running out of time."

"Hey, your mom isn't going to freak out or anything, is she?"

"Don't worry about it," I said, trying to reassure us both.

"You're the boss."

Joe opened the container of dye and began rubbing the contents into my hair.

"Did you know green was the sacred color of the Aztecs?" he asked.

"How do you even know this stuff?"

"I read books," Joe said. "You should try it."

"You're hilarious."

We waited in my room for the dye to set in. I worked on a zine while Joe drew in his sketch pad. We took turns picking music to play.

"Gonna start working on my comic zine," he said, holding up a page on which he'd sketched thumbnails of an eight-page comic.

I gave him the thumbs-up.

When the timer on my phone finally went off, Joe hopped up.

"Time to rinse," he said. "Here's hoping your hair actually looks green."

We headed back into the bathroom, where I bent my head over the side of the tub. But we didn't get a chance to start rinsing before I heard the front door open.

"Malú, are you here?"

"Oh, no, my mom," I said. "I didn't think she'd be back so early."

"I think we've been caught . . . green-handed?" Joe said.

"Don't joke," I said. "In the bathroom," I called out to Mom. I heard her make her way down the creaky-floored hallway, each step counting down to what would surely be an epic Mom freak-out.

"¡Ave María purísima!" she said when she appeared in the doorway.

I knew it was bad when Mom got religious and invoked the Virgin Mary. She looked around the bathroom, taking in the damage.

"What have you two done?"

Joe sat on the toilet lid; locks of my hair covered the floor around his sneakers. What was left of my hair was tucked into a plastic shower cap, though not tucked in enough to keep it from drip, drip, dripping. A splotch of green dye landed on my shoe. Mom looked at my shoe, then at me. Only then did I notice the green everywhere. On our hands, on my shirt, on the sink, on the floor.

The container of Neon Iguana hair dye sat on a ring of green on top of the toilet tank, a little too close to the toilet paper doll Señora Oralia had given us. While her lemon-yellow skirt was spared, the doll attached to it was not as lucky. I thought it was an improvement on her overall look, but based on Mom's reaction, she didn't agree.

"Out!" Mom said.

"But, Mom, I need to rinse this off!"

I pointed to my head, afraid to touch it for fear of making contact with the hair dye and spreading more green.

"Not you," she said. "I think it's time for you to leave, Joe."

Joe flashed her a sheepish smile as he gathered a pair of rubber gloves, a plastic bowl, and the half-empty container of hair dye into a shopping bag.

"Bye, Señora Morales," he said.

"Good-bye, Joe," Mom said in her I-am-not-at-all-happy tone.

"See you at school in a little while," he called back to me as he headed out the door. "If you-know-who lets you out, of course."

He looked at Mom and wiggled his eyebrows.

"You're cleaning this up, señorita," Mom said. She left the bathroom and came back holding a dustpan in one hand and a broom in the other. The look on her face was one of surprise, as if she were seeing my hair for the first time.

"I can't believe you left all your hair on the floor," Mom said.

She kicked a clump of hair with her shoe before turning

her attention to the rest of the bathroom.

"Ay, Malú," she said. "Look at this mess."

She looked at the towel I held, formerly solid yellow now with faded green splotches. There were a couple more stained towels from the matching set lying in a pile on the radiator cover.

"What possessed you to do this?" she asked. After assessing the floor situation, I had to agree with Mom. It did look like I had left all my hair on the floor. I figured now wasn't the best time to tell her about the band, and that I couldn't be in a punk band with my little-kid braids.

"Clean all of this up," she said. "Including yourself."

Mom left the bathroom, and I got to work. I swept until all the hair was in the trash and I scrubbed the green dye off surfaces as much as possible.

When I was finished, I undressed and stepped into the tub, letting the warm water run over me. Rivers of green trickled down. They mixed with the water and swirled at the bottom of the tub like little green eddies before being rushed down the drain. I scrubbed my neck hard to try to get all the tiny pieces of hair off.

Finally, when the water ran mostly clear, I climbed out. I wiped condensation from the mirror and looked at myself. My bangs weren't the same shade of green as the Neon Iguana hair dye in the jar, but they were green.

"Awesome." I grinned at the me I saw reflected.

Quetzal's
guide
to
DYEING YOUR HAIR!

- Lives in the cloud forest in Central America.

- Blue-green feathers on wings, tail, and crest and scarlet feathers on its breast.

- Tail feathers of male birds were used by rulers and priests in Aztec and Maya cultures. The tail feathers can grow up to 3 feet long!

QUETZAL'S TIP #1:

Pick the brightest and most beautifully weird color!

Quetzals are not endangered but they are threatened. Save the Quetzal!

Quetzal Green!

Resplendent Red!

Cloud Forest Blue!

QUETZAL'S TIP #2:

Dark hair will have to be . . . bleached! This can take a while and involves chemicals so you may want to have a book handy.

QUETZAL'S TIP #3:

Some things you may want to have on hand . . .

Didn't work for me, but maybe that's because Mom buys "all natural" toothpaste. Does leave you smelling MINTY FRESH, though!

We interrupt this guide to present . . .

THINGS TO SAY TO YOUR PARENTS WHEN THEY FLIP OUT!

It's only <u>SEMI</u> permanent!

I thought this was <u>YOUR</u> favorite color!

Now you'll never lose me in a crowd!

And now back to business!

QUETZAL'S TIP #4:

Remove everything you don't want to risk staining from the area. Seriously.

Cover the floors with newspaper if you can. And don't use the good towels!

Good luck with your **RAD NEW HAIR!**

Your hard work is about to pay off.
M

Chapter 33

"Why are you knitting?" I asked.

Mom sat on the couch with her yarn monster. She looked up from her needles with a frown.

"Because I feel like it."

"Uh-uh," I said. "You only knit when something's up."

"You think you know me pretty well, don't you?"

I shrugged. "I know that scarf is a sign that something's up," I said.

"Maybe I'm knitting to stay calm," she said. "What is this about?" She pointed to my head with a knitting needle. "Is this part of your rebellious stage?"

"I'm not rebelling, Mom," I said, even though maybe I was doing that too. "I like the way my hair looks."

I pulled my fingers through my wet bangs and ran my

hand over my head. It felt soft, like a piece of velvet.

"Anyway, it's just hair," I said.

"Sí," Mom said. "That's exactly what your dad would say. Just hair. Just clothes."

"What's wrong with my clothes?" I asked. "This morning you said I looked nice."

I'd changed back into the outfit I'd picked out for Fall Fiesta and thrown on an old oversized red cardigan that belonged to Dad. Before coming out of the bathroom, I'd consulted a cool photo of Teresa Covarrubias that I'd printed out. I'd lined my eyes in the same dark cat-eye style, applied a dark lipstick, and gelled my hair so that it was kind of spiky on top with bangs over one eye. Mom was already mad about the hair, so I might as well finish the look.

"You know who you look like?" Mom said. "La Chilindrina. With green hair. No, wait. I know. You look like the child of la Chilindrina and Nosferatu!"

For a minute Mom forgot her anger and laughed at her own joke.

"You remember la Chilindrina, right? She was on that show you used to watch with your abuelo."

"I remember her," I said. La Chilindrina always wore a red sweater twisted in the back—like she couldn't figure out how to dress herself—thick, black-framed glasses, and her hair in two ponytails. "And that is probably the meanest thing you've ever said to me."

"That's who you two are, you and Joe," Mom said.

"La Chilindrina and el Chavo del Ocho. A couple of troublemakers."

She laughed even harder.

"That's not funny, Mom."

Mom tried to talk but couldn't because she was laughing so hard.

"Okay, I'm glad you find it amusing," I said. "Why can't you be cool like Dad?"

I looked at her sitting there, long hair cascading over her shoulders. She wore a purple rebozo over a T-shirt and jeans. Her legs were crossed, and a brown leather sandal dangled off her big toe. I could not see how my parents were ever together. Mom was obviously from an entirely different planet than me and Dad.

She finally stopped laughing and took a breath.

"One of us has to be the uncool, mature one," she said, dropping her knitting into the bag next to the couch.

I crossed my arms and waited for her tell me what my punishment would be, hoping she wouldn't ground me and forbid me from going to Fall Fiesta.

"I need you to walk Señora Oralia to Fall Fiesta," Mom said, wiping tears from her eyes. "Do you think you can do that?"

"Yes!" I said with more excitement than I might have under other circumstances. "So . . . I can still go?"

"Yes, you may go," Mom said.

"Are *you* going to Fall Fiesta?" I asked, careful not to push my luck.

"I don't know," Mom said. "I brought papers home to grade, so we'll see how much I can get done in the next couple of hours."

"And you aren't mad about my hair?"

"Oh, I'm still mad," she said, getting up. "But you're the one who has to walk around looking like a green-haired Chilindrina. I hope you don't give Señora Oralia a heart attack."

Mom laughed as she walked away, but I was too relieved I wasn't going to miss the show to get upset about her jokes.

I went to my room, where I scooped up my worry dolls and put them in a pocket of my bag. Then I took a picture of myself to send to Dad. By the time I came out of my room, Mom was already in the hallway, chatting with Señora Oralia.

"Here she is," Mom said. "Your colorful escort."

"Pelo verde," Señora Oralia said with a laugh. "Ah, nothing these children do surprises me anymore."

"Well, I'm glad," Mom said. "Malú, help Señora Oralia down the stairs. Hopefully, I'll see you in a little while."

Hopefully not, I thought as Señora Oralia and I hooked arms and walked carefully down the stairs.

"Tell me, why do you kids do that to your hair?" Señora Oralia asked. "I don't understand."

I thought about Señora Oralia's question, and about my asking Joe earlier why he'd dyed his hair blue.

"I don't know," I said. "I like the way it looks. Plus, I don't want to look like everyone else. I like being unique."

"But you look like everyone else who colors their hair some bright color, ¿no?" she asked.

"Yeah, I guess," I said.

Señora Oralia shook her head. "No entiendo," she said. "I don't understand why you kids try so hard to stick out."

"It's hard to explain." I said. "I just know that I like my hair like this. It makes me feel good. Like I'm being me."

"Bueno, if you're happy, and you aren't hurting anyone, who cares?"

"What do you think of my hair, Señora Oralia?" I asked.

"¿La verdad?"

"Yes, the truth," I said.

"I would have picked purple myself," she replied, and touched her hair. "¿Qué piensas?"

"I think you'd look cool with purple hair," I said.

"You know what you look like?" I waited for her to laugh at me like Mom did. "You look like un pajarito quetzal."

She gave me a wink. Somehow Señora Oralia had known that was exactly the look I was going for.

Chapter 34

After I dropped off Señora Oralia in the auditorium, I went back outside to wait for the band. The parking lot of Posada Middle School looked like an autumn wonderland. It was decorated with bales of hay and pumpkins and red and orange balloons. Long banners of colorful papel picado hung overhead. There was an impressive food and drink table. Ms. Anderson, the art teacher, poured pink sugar into a cotton candy machine. I watched as it slowly turned into pink spiderwebs.

"Wow, what happened to your hair, María Luisa?" Selena sauntered up, and her eyes got wide as she looked at my hair.

The hypnotic whirl of the cotton candy machine helped

keep my full-on panic about our secret show at bay. The last person I wanted to see was Selena.

"Did you fall into some toxic sludge?" she asked, wrinkling her nose.

"Do you fall into toxic sludge every morning?" I asked, wrinkling my nose back at her.

Today Selena wore a long fuchsia skirt and a white off-the-shoulder blouse embroidered along the neckline with flowers. Her hair was up in a fancy crown of braids. She had on bright red lipstick and blush, and her eyes were made up. She didn't look like she'd just fallen into toxic sludge. She looked like she came to dance and take care of business.

Ms. Anderson held out two paper cones topped with pink sugar clouds.

"No, thank you," I said. My stomach couldn't handle food right then. But Selena grabbed hers and bit into it.

"You know hair dye is against the dress code," Selena said.

"Of course I know that," I said. "Don't worry about me and the dress code."

"That's too bad your little talent show plans fell through, huh?" she asked, giving me a big red smirk. A little piece of cotton candy stuck to her lipstick.

Nerves and anger bubbled up inside me like someone had poured vinegar into a science-project volcano full of baking soda.

"And it's too bad your Irish dance class didn't happen," I said. "It's a bummer your mom said no."

I didn't know why I'd said that, but it had come out of my mouth like . . . toxic sludge. As soon as I'd said it, I felt terrible. Especially when I saw Selena's face. She looked like I'd smacked her. I could see her chewing on the inside of her lower lip. Finally she opened her mouth to say something, but nothing came out. She turned on her heel and started to walk away.

Before I knew it, I found myself speed walking to catch up with her.

"Wait!" I called out.

She stopped but didn't turn around. I dug into my bag until I found what I was looking for.

"Here," I said. I handed her one of the few copies of our talent show flyer that I'd saved.

"What's this?" she asked, looking at it. "I mean, I know what it is, but why are you giving it to me?"

"We're still going to do our show," I said. "Joe's mom is going to help us. And if you want, you can be part of it too."

"Why would I do that?" Selena asked. "I'm already in the talent show. The *real* talent show."

"I know," I said, and shrugged. "But if you decide you want to do something different, maybe something you've always wanted to do but felt like you couldn't, that's what the Alterna-Fiesta show is about."

Selena looked at the flyer, then up at me. She didn't suck her teeth or swat me away. She was quiet and hard to read.

"Never mind," I said. "Keep it or throw it away. Whatever."

I didn't know what else to say, so I walked away, back toward the band's planned meeting spot. I watched as Selena folded the flyer and stuck it into the pocket of her skirt before going inside the auditorium.

Chapter 35

"It's showtime," Joe said, trotting up. "Oooh, cotton candy!"

A large black mariachi hat hung around his neck from a strap.

"What is *that*?" I asked, pointing to it.

"What does it look like?" Joe asked. "Dude, you have no idea how hard it was to keep this thing from getting smashed. It's so big."

He pulled the hat onto his head.

"You're not serious," I said.

Benny walked up with Ellie in tow. Both of them wore matching mariachi hats.

"You planned this and didn't tell me?"

"Are you mad?" Joe asked.

"Or just jealous?" Benny asked, and they both laughed.

"Well, yeah," I said.

"No worries." Ellie had been hiding a similar hat behind her back, and she placed it on my head. "Did you think we'd leave you out?"

"That totally completes your look," Joe said.

"You should've seen your face when you thought you weren't getting a hat," Benny said, playfully shoving me.

"Whatever," I said.

I caught our reflection in the glass wall. Joe with his Henry Huggins look, tall Benny with his long hair and trumpet case, Ellie with her army jacket covered in pins, her long red hair sticking out from under her hat, and me. A group of outsider weirdos in matching T-shirts and mariachi hats. We looked ridiculous and amazing at the same time.

"We can't bring these into the auditorium," I said. "The four of us in mariachi hats would definitely sound an alarm."

We dropped the hats off in the library then filed into the auditorium with kids and parents to watch some of the principal-approved talent show before meeting up with Mrs. Hidalgo.

Principal Rivera walked onto the stage and welcomed the audience to what she called a "very special celebration." She went on to explain how on this thirtieth anniversary of the school it was important to remember Posada the man as someone who proudly represented

Mexican people and culture through his art. She showed some slides of his prints, including the really famous one of a skeleton woman wearing a big hat.

"I'm sure Posada would be proud of our students who are performing today," Principal Rivera concluded, "most of them representing Mexican culture. Please give them your undivided attention and enjoy today's show." She clapped, and the audience joined in as the lights dimmed.

"Did anyone else just suddenly become nervous?" Joe whispered when the first performer came onto the stage.

"Yeah," I said, watching the kid play the violin. "I'm about to be sick."

"Don't get sick on us," Benny said. He pulled a candy bar from the pocket of his jacket and unwrapped it.

"How can you even eat right now?" I asked.

"I'm hungry." Benny shrugged. "Want a bite?"

I stuck out my tongue like I was gagging.

"Aw, come on," Ellie said. "You guys aren't really nervous, are you?"

"Yeah, this is going to be fun," Benny said.

"Fun. Right." I slumped in my seat to watch the show.

An eighth grader sang a familiar song. Her voice cracked when she first opened her mouth. I knew the feeling well.

"What if that happens to me?" I whispered to Ellie.

"Don't freak out," she said. "You're going to be great."

The girl got through her song, but she rushed off the stage near tears. I swallowed hard as I watched Mrs. Larson meet her at the edge of the backstage area.

When it was Selena's turn, she walked out, straight-backed, hands holding her skirt so it was on full display. She didn't look nervous at all, like this was something she did all the time. I remembered all the awards at the dance school. Then the jumpy familiar guitar sounds of "La bamba" started.

"My song," Joe said excitedly.

For the next few minutes we watched as Selena twirled and dipped and stomped along to the music, always with a big smile on her face. If this was a movie, she would have broken a heel and run off the stage, mortified. But this wasn't a movie. She made it through the entire song without a problem. At the end, she even took off her candy necklace and tossed it into the audience. Kids jumped out of their seats and scrambled to grab it like she was some kind of rock star.

With the end of each performance, my tongue felt more and more like it was made out of cardboard. Finally Joe nudged me.

"Just got a text from my mom," he said. "She's outside with our stuff. Time to set up."

Chapter 36

This definitely wasn't Mrs. Hidalgo's first time setting up a DIY show. She was a pro. We didn't have a stage, but we had power. With Mr. Baca's help, she found a spot for us outside the school, near one of the cafeteria exits. She and Joe unloaded the drum kit from the Hidalgos' basement. Mr. Baca connected extension cords into electrical outlets inside the cafeteria that Mrs. Hidalgo ran out to where we were setting up.

"Whatever happens," Mr. Baca said to us conspiratorially, "I was never here."

He winked and disappeared inside the cafeteria.

"As long as they don't decide to pull the plug, we're good," Mrs. Hidalgo said.

I tried not to think about throwing up as I watched

people start to come out of the auditorium. The talent show must have just ended.

"You okay, Malú?" Mrs. Hidalgo came over and handed me a water bottle.

It's going to be fine, I repeated in my head as I gulped. I wiped my mouth and shook off my nerves.

"I don't know if I can do this," I whispered.

"It's okay to feel anxious," Mrs. Hidalgo said. "Anyone would be."

In the distance I could see Principal Rivera by the school's entrance. She wore jeans, which almost made her look like a regular person.

"What do you think she's going to do?" I asked, knowing it wasn't punk to worry about Principal Rivera's reaction, and feeling embarrassed.

"Well, you don't have to do it," Mrs. Hidalgo said.

I looked over at Ellie and Joe, who were fiddling with their instruments. Benny silently played the notes of the song on the buttons of his trumpet.

"Maybe you should think about why you wanted to do this, and then decide," Mrs. Hidalgo said. "I'm going to set up the mics. Just in case." She patted my arm.

"Oh, almost forgot," Mrs. Hidalgo turned back and dug around in her bag. "Hope you've got a CD player and not just a Walkman." She handed me a square envelope.

"Thanks," I said. Inside the envelope was a CD and a playlist. I sat down on the curb and thought about why we planned the alternative talent show. Because Principal

Rivera excluded us from the Fall Fiesta talent show for being too loud and not being good enough for the anniversary show. I thought about it more, and I knew there were other reasons. Reasons that involved Mom and feeling like I could never be who she wanted me to be.

Oz tells the Cowardly Lion that real courage is facing danger when you are afraid. I was afraid. No, I was terrified. But the talent show and the song were my idea, and I couldn't back out now. Suddenly the feelings of uncertainty about doing the show disappeared, like someone had taken an eraser to writing on a chalkboard. I walked to where the rest of the band waited by the drum kit. Ellie sat behind it ready to rock.

"Ready, Freddy?" Joe asked. He bounced around, shaking his shoulders like a boxer getting ready for a match.

I chewed on my nails and wished I had my headphones to drown out the sounds around me.

"No," I said. "But let's do this."

"Here we go," Joe said, "the Co-Co's on three."

The four of us piled our hands together. Mine wasn't the only clammy one.

"One, two, three," we said in unison. "The Co-Co's!" Hands together, hands apart. I silently wished for the confidence of all my favorite punk singers, and even of Lola B, to get me through the performance.

Chapter 37

I walked up to the microphone stand Mrs. Hidalgo had set up for me and tapped it. The sound echoed around the parking lot.

"Hello, Posada Middle School," I said hesitantly.

Some kids had come over while we were setting up. Other kids and adults started to trickle in to see what was going on.

"So, we're the Co-Co's," I said. "We tried out for the Fall Fiesta talent show, but we didn't get in because we were terrible."

People laughed, and I felt myself relax a little.

"Actually, we didn't get in because we were too loud. And because we played a punk rock song, and punk apparently has nothing to do with this celebration of Posada, the school or the person."

Someone in the crowd booed. But not *at* us. I think he was booing *for* us.

"But you know what?" I said, my voice getting louder. "José Guadalupe Posada was totally punk." I saw Mr. Baca in the crowd making the rock-and-roll sign with his hand. "Principal Rivera said Posada represented Mexican people and culture, but what she didn't tell you is that he represented *all* people, especially the ones who needed a voice and a way to be heard."

There was a murmur in the crowd. I looked at Mrs. Hidalgo, who smiled at me and nodded. Señora Oralia stood next to her. She smiled too.

"I read a book about him that I got from our school library, and I learned that he criticized stuff that was wrong with the government and things that were unfair in society. And he did it through his art. What's more punk than that?" I asked. I looked at the faces that had gathered closely. My classmates were listening to what I had to say. Some were nodding in agreement.

"So we're doing the Alterna-Fiesta talent show for Posada and for us and for anyone else who got left out of the talent show because they didn't fit in. Anyone who wants to perform can come up after our set. Everyone gets a voice here no matter how weird or loud or untraditional you are."

I took a big gulp of air and looked over at Joe.

"We're the Co-Co's," Joe said into his microphone as we'd planned. "And this is not your abuela's music!"

Ellie struck her drumsticks together to count us off.

Benny played the opening notes of the traditional song, and the four of us sang a slow, bellowing chorus. We did our best to imitate the mournful-sounding ranchera singers we'd listened to at Calaca. And then we launched into the fastest and loudest rendition of "Cielito lindo" anyone at Posada Middle School—and probably the world—had ever heard.

When it was my turn to sing alone, I closed my eyes and took a deep breath as if I were preparing to jump into the deepest end of a swimming pool. As I sang, I kept my eyes closed, too afraid to see the faces looking back at me. Every nerve in my body was alive and buzzing. I imagined I was Lola B singing to a sold-out stadium. I pictured Selena in the audience, her jaw on the floor.

Joe, Ellie, and Benny joined me for the chorus, which says that singing makes a sad heart happy. And I knew it was true, because any sadness I felt about leaving home or about Selena and Mom didn't exist in that moment.

Hearing the band sing together always made me want to giggle, so I did. Getting a good laugh out made me feel more at ease. I sang, clutching the microphone so hard, my hand hurt.

When I finally got the nerve to open my eyes, I looked into the crowd of Posada kids, teachers, and families that had gathered. I spotted familiar faces: Señor Ascencio, Selena and Diana, Mr. Jackson, and Principal Rivera. She had a confused look on her face, like she didn't know what to make of us or the situation. And then I saw familiar faces that I didn't expect to see. I thought my eyes were playing tricks on me.

When I looked back to where Mrs. Hidalgo and Señora Oralia were, they'd been joined by Mom and . . . Dad! Mom's lips moved, singing along with the words, like we were singing together. Maybe this was the best way to share my secret project with her after all.

Someone in the audience let out a loud mariachi cry, and Joe replied with his own. Ellie's hands were a blur as she banged on the drums so hard, her red mane flailing like flames all around her. Benny swung his trumpet from left to right, his ponytail following along. With that, I shed the last of my nervousness like a snake's skin.

For the rest of our performance, I pogoed and twirled, and the lyrics didn't stumble awkwardly out of my mouth like they sometimes did when I spoke Spanish. They flowed like they had always been part of me.

I looked in Mom's direction. What did she think as we turned "Cielito lindo" upside down? She caught my eye and smiled.

When the band played the final note of the song, I took off my mariachi hat and, like Selena with her candy necklace, tossed it into the crowd. I realized it probably wasn't the best idea because this hat was about fifty times bigger and way heavier than a candy necklace.

The saucerlike hat soared over the student body. Kids grabbed at it until an eighth grader emerged with it on his head.

We got a loud round of applause and whooping from

the crowd and, as we'd practiced, we held hands and took a group bow. And even though there was no stage to dive off, Joe stood on one of our little amps and leaped into the crowd, where he was caught by some of Selena's candy crew. Maybe Joe was punk after all.

Chapter 38

"That was awesome!" Ellie said, jumping around. It was the most excited I'd ever seen her. "That was better than—"

"An A plus on a test?" Benny asked.

"Let me think about it," Ellie said with a grin.

"I can't wait to do it again," Joe said.

My body shook like when I didn't listen to Mom and had two cups of coffee with sugar in a row. I waited for Principal Rivera to come find us. We had a T-shirt ready and waiting for her. But she was busy with a couple of sixth-grade boys who had taken over the microphones and were doing a comedy routine. One pretended to be a ventriloquist while the other one was the dummy. Who knew there were so many jokes about farts?

Out of the corner of my eye I saw Selena approaching,

but I was too happy and too drained of energy to move. And part of me didn't care what she was going to say anyway.

"I have to say, María Luisa, I wasn't expecting that."

"What?"

"*You* singing in Spanish," she said, swishing her long skirt left and right.

"Why do you think I don't know Spanish?" I asked. "And why do you care so much?"

"I was just trying to give you a compliment, okay?" she said. "I was going to tell you that it was kind of weird. Okay, it was really weird. But it wasn't so bad."

I felt too good to let Selena bring me down, so I just gave her the most genuine smile I could muster.

"Your compliments need a little work," I said. "But thanks."

Selena looked at me like a cat eyeing its prey, then walked off, her long skirt sweeping the floor. She didn't end up taking the stage after us, but I hoped she would get to take those Irish dance lessons she wanted.

Principal Rivera announced that the school would consider having an "open mic" at next year's Fall Fiesta but that, unfortunately, she had to disconnect the microphones. A group of kids booed until Ellie got us going on a protest chant.

"What do we want?" she yelled.

"Alterna-Fiesta," the group responded, with me, Benny, and Joe taking the lead.

"When do we want it?"

"Now!"

We kept it going for a minute before kids started to wander away toward food and games. I saw Mrs. Hidalgo go over to Principal Rivera. I hoped she could smooth things over for us, but if she couldn't, that was okay too.

"Surprise!" a familiar voice called out.

Dad rushed toward me and scooped me up in a hug. Mom followed, carrying a bunch of flowers.

"You guys were *amazing*," he said.

"I can't believe you're here." I hugged him as tight as I could for fear that he'd disappear again, and breathed in his familiar Dad smell. "I'm sorry."

"What are you sorry about?" Dad asked, looking confused.

"For making you feel bad," I said. "About Mrs. Hidalgo."

"Lú, you know I wish I always had the answers you need. Obviously, I don't. But I'm glad you've met someone who seems to get you like Mrs. Hidalgo does," Dad said, and smiled. "Really. And I can't wait to meet her."

"Me too," I said, relieved.

When I pulled away from Dad, Mom grabbed me in her own tight squeeze.

"Dad's right," she said, standing back. "You were amazing."

"What are you . . . ? What are both of you doing here?"

"I wouldn't miss this for anything," Mom said, holding out the cluster of flowers. They looked like the flowers tattooed on Mrs. Hidalgo's arm. "For the singer."

"Thanks, Mom," I said.

"They're dahlias," Mom said. "The national flower of Mexico."

I almost said, *Of course they are, SuperMexican,* but instead I just said, "These are really pretty."

"Why didn't you tell me about this?" she asked.

Mom's face sported a look I call sad-mad. Her eyes looked sad, but her scrunched forehead looked mad. I guess now I knew why Mom had acted so weird this morning.

Dad started to back away.

"I'll leave you to talk," he said. "There's a caramel apple calling out to me."

Mom nodded, and Dad headed toward the carnival.

"Well?" Mom asked. "Is this what you've been doing with Joe all this time? Why didn't you tell me?"

"Why do you think, Mom? I figured the last thing you'd want to do was watch me be your weirdo daughter. Especially in front of a crowd."

"Malú, we have our differences, but did you actually think I would want to miss you do something like this?" Mom asked. "Talk to me. What's up?"

I stared at the ground and rolled a small rock back and forth under my shoe.

"I guess I just didn't want to hear you criticize everything like you usually do. My Spanish or my clothes," I said. "I get enough of that from Selena at school."

"Selena?"

"Yeah, Mom," I said. "I know it's hard to believe, but we aren't friends. My friends are the band. We're all pretty different, but they don't make fun of me."

"I'm sorry, Malú," Mom said. "I know moving here has been hard enough. And I'm glad you've made friends. I never meant to make you feel bad about yourself."

"Well, you do," I said. "You always look down on stuff I like doing because I'm not being a señorita or not appreciating my culture. It's hard for me to figure out how to be me when you're always telling me it's wrong. I hate that you're always disappointed in me."

"I'm not disappointed in you, Malú," Mom said. "And I'm sorry if I've made you feel that way."

"I can't help it that my Spanish stinks," I said. "And I like my green hair."

Mom nodded like she was really listening. "I guess I didn't realize I was being so hard on you."

"Not always," I said, realizing Mom felt pretty bad. "But sometimes."

"Well, Mrs. Hidalgo told me about the show. And your dad mentioned it," she said. "Seemed like everyone knew except for me. And I had to wonder why that was. I guess sometimes we project feelings about ourselves onto others, and I'm sorry if I've done that to you."

"What do you mean, Mom?"

"Well, it's not a coincidence that I do what I do for a living," she said. "You know, growing up, I never felt like I was enough of anything either, or too much of what I wasn't supposed to be. Not Mexican enough, too nerdy."

"You?" I asked in disbelief. "SuperMexican?"

"When your dad told me about the band and about how

you've been feeling, it made me stop to think about how I've acted," she said. "Even this morning. I couldn't help freaking out about your hair. Guess I have to work on letting you be you. And being less uncool."

"You're not uncool, Mom," I said. "You're just . . . you're just you."

Mom laughed. "I know I don't always show it, but I love that you have no problem being an individual no matter what others think," Mom said. "Not even me. That's not an easy thing to do."

"So, you don't mind the hair after all?" I asked.

"Do I have to like the hair?"

"I guess not," I said. "But can you stop bugging me about being more of a señorita? Or at least let me decide what that means?"

"I'll try," Mom said.

"So . . . be honest, what did you think of the song?"

"That was, by far, the most unique version of 'Cielito lindo' I've ever heard," Mom said.

"You thought it was terrible, right?"

"Unique doesn't mean terrible," Mom said. "You of all people should know that. I thought it was great. I love what you guys did with it, mixing the old and the new."

"Thanks, Mom."

"I'm proud of you for singing in Spanish too," she said. "I know that must have been nerve-racking."

"Actually," I said. "It wasn't as hard as I thought it would be."

"I'm glad to hear that," Mom said. "You know, you might

be on your way to becoming SuperMexican Jr. with that singing."

We couldn't hold in our laughter at that.

"What's so funny, ladies?" Joe asked, coming up to us, his mariachi hat back to hanging around his neck.

"Inside joke," I said.

"Hey, Manolito's has a food truck here," Joe said. "They have the best tacos. You in, María Luisa . . . I mean, Malú?"

"You can call me María Luisa if you want," I said. "I don't mind."

Joe shook his head. "Make up your mind, dude."

"Yes," Mom said. "We're definitely in. Let's go find your dad."

Chapter 39

"I should've totally smashed my guitar," Joe said.

"You would have to put in a lot more hours at Calaca to buy a new one," Mrs. Hidalgo replied. "Maybe you can save that for when you're touring and making the big bucks."

"Yeah," Joe said. "You're probably right, Ma."

We sat at a picnic table next to Manolito's food truck, sharing baskets of tortilla chips and salsa. I'd ordered a vegetarian taco, and Mom had even made sure to ask them to leave off the cilantro without adding a comment about my lack of Mexican taste buds.

Joe and his parents, Mom and Dad, Benny and Ellie, and even Señora Oralia joined us. I was excited to finally introduce Dad to Mrs. Hidalgo. I knew he'd like her and understand why she was so important to me. I had all my favorite people in the same place, and it made me feel like I was home. Even if it wasn't the home I'd left a couple of months earlier.

"So, how does it feel to be the singer in a punk band?" Dad asked.

"It feels pretty great," I said.

"Your friends seem cool," he added.

I looked over at Joe, Benny, and Ellie, who were blowing straw wrappers at each other. *My friends.* I might have actually found my Yellow-Brick-Road posse.

"Yeah, they are," I said.

"Are the Co-Co's going to be a punk ranchera band?" Mr. Hidalgo asked. "I like it."

"Nah," Joe said. "Maybe we'll write our own songs, right?"

I nodded. If we were going to be a real band, we had to start writing our own music.

"Bueno, I liked the song," Señora Oralia said. "María Luisa, eres la grande pequeña."

"Yes, she is," Mom said. "Small in size but big in voice."

I felt myself blushing.

"Your hair looks great, by the way," Mrs. Hidalgo whispered.

"Thanks. My mom doesn't think so," I said. "Lucky for her I have to dye it back by Monday."

"Going from brown to green *is* a little extreme," she said. "Might just take some getting used to."

"Yeah, maybe." I ran my hand through my hair.

"She seemed to enjoy your performance," Mrs. Hidalgo said with a smile.

"Yeah," I said. "But what if she always thinks of me as her weirdo pie-chart kid who doesn't meet any of her expectations?"

"Don't worry about that so much," Mrs. Hidalgo said. "You know, Malú, I like to think of us as more like patchwork quilts," Mrs. Hidalgo said. "Some pieces are prettier than others. Some pieces match and some don't. But if you remove a square, you're just left with an incomplete quilt, and who wants that? All our pieces are equally important if they make us whole. Even the weird ones."

I felt really lucky to have met Mrs. Hidalgo. She made me feel like there was hope. Even for little weirdo coconuts like me. I hoped to grow up to be at least half as rad as her.

✂✂✂

After dinner I holed up in my room to work on a zine before bed. Dad and I made plans to check out Laurie's Planet of Sound and some other nearby record stores the next morning, so I knew I shouldn't stay up too late. I washed off my makeup, put on my pajama pants, but kept on my Co-Co's shirt. I pulled out the mix Mrs. Hidalgo had made for me and put on my headphones, turning the volume up loud, the only way to listen to punk rock.

Like Dorothy from *The Wizard of Oz*, I definitely wasn't in Kansas anymore. But Chicago had started to feel less and less like Oz. I realized it was possible to make it feel more like home.

As the music flowed through my headphones, I thought about what Mrs. Hidalgo had said at dinner. I knew I was part of Mom and part of Dad, but also part of things that were neither of them. I was my own patchwork quilt.

Even punk music felt more like a mismatched quilt than I had ever considered. Being punk meant a lot of different things, just like being Mexican meant many things. Sometimes those things didn't seem to match. And that was okay because I'd discovered that maybe the first rule of punk was to make your own rules.

THE FIRST RULE OF PUNK

BE
THE
Real
YOU

Sometimes BOLD and BRAVE and wanting to be inside the frame.
BINGHAM'S BEST BRAND
Sometimes SCARED and UNSURE and happy to be outside the frame.

A half-Mexican

GIRL

who . . .

* hates cilantro. *

* struggles with español. *

* is still learning about her culture. *

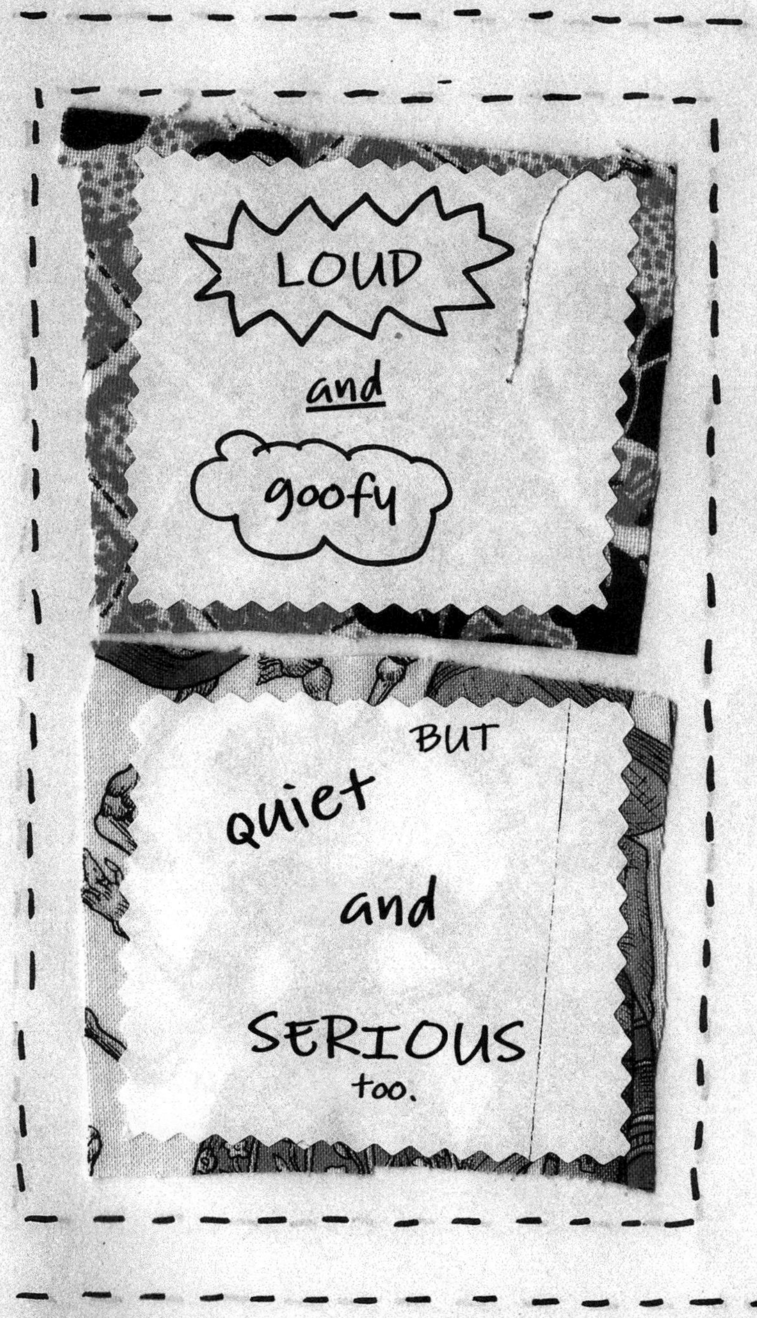
LOUD
and
goofy
BUT
quiet
and
SERIOUS
too.

weird
punky
musical
HEART
artistic
sarcastic
FREE

Modern
daughter hija
amiga
friend
María Luisa
Malú

MisMAtChED MUsic
Posada's Calavera con guitarra
"Swift Moves" -The Brat
"La bamba" -Richie Valens
"Volver, volver" -Piñata Protest
"Poder elegir" -Downtown Boys
"Come On, Let's Go" -Girl in a Coma
"Cielito lindo" -Lola Beltrán
"Soy yo" -Bomba Estéreo

DONE
your
way
M

How to Make a Zine!

1. Fold the paper in half, then into quarters, and one more time into eighths.

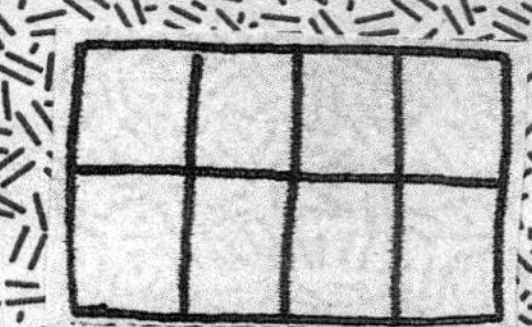

cut at the fold

2. Open your paper so that it is folded in half. Cut halfway across the middle from the fold.

3. Open the paper and fold it lengthwise along the crease with the cut. Then hold it at either end and push the sections in toward each other.

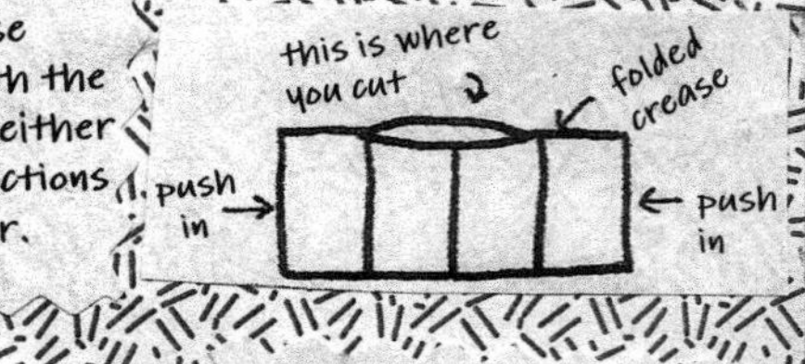

back cover

your blank soon-to-be ZINE!

front cover

4. Voilà! You should have a little booklet. Now you just need to fill in the pages with all your great ideas!

Acknowledgments, or People Who Led to This Book

There is a memoir by the playwright Adrienne Kennedy titled *People Who Led to My Plays* in which she details, in the form of annotated lists, the people, things, experiences, and memories that influenced her work. It gives a sense of how everything and anything can alter one's view of the world, spark an idea, leave an impression, and lead to something else. This is nowhere near an exhaustive list of who and what led to this book, but it's a start.

Stefanie Von Borstel, my agent, thank you for seeing something special in my story and for taking a chance on me. I am proud to know you and to be affiliated with the work you do through Full Circle Literary. Joanna Cárdenas, my editor, your enthusiasm, intelligence, humor, and support transformed my manuscript. Thank you for pushing me to dig deeper. You are a gift, and none of this could have been possible without you. Kat Fajardo, a talented artist doing important work, thank you for bringing Malú and her spunkiness to life on the book jacket. In an industry that struggles to be inclusive, one of the things I'm most proud of is having this team of Latinas be part of the creation of this book.

Ken Wright, Kate Renner, Dana Li, Kaitlin Severini, Abigail Powers, and everyone at Viking Children's Books (Penguin Random House) whose hands, hearts, and minds have been a part of this journey, thank you for helping to make this happen.

Taylor Martindale and Adriana Dominguez at Full Circle for support and for the good work they do to bring diverse stories to the world.

Jenna Freedman, who not only read an early draft and gave her much-valued feedback, but also is my BFF in zines, librarianship, and life. Thomas Pace, who read and posed questions that made me think about where I wanted this story to go, and who didn't laugh even though our friendship consists of constant snark.

My high school English teachers, especially Cristina Bascuas, my eleventh grade creative writing teacher, who believed I was a writer before I did. The Niggli-Moores and Karen Larson for their friendship and for always being so supportive of my writing projects. Christopher Lamlamay and Thomas Matthews, my favorite neighbors, who opened their door to me and my various technological needs while I worked on this book. You are lifesavers! Jessica Mills, who not only knew that "Blitzkrieg Bop" is the easiest Ramones song to learn but also was the first female punk musician I ever saw perform in person. You're still the coolest. Travis Fristoe, who showed me the power and magic of zines at a time when I needed it most. How I wish I could share this with you.

Lucia Gonzalez, Oralia Garza de Cortes, Ruth Tobar, Lettycia Terrones, Sandra Rios Balderrama, and all the REFORMA–CAYASC librarian activists who champion Latino kid lit and are persistent, take-no-mess voices in the world, your work and dedication inspire me.

In *Nepantla: Essays from the Land in the Middle,* Pat Mora refers to the authors who have influenced her as "unseen teachers." There are so many writers and illustrators who have influenced me over my lifetime as a reader, but there is a special place in my heart for Michele Serros, Sandra Cisneros, and Jaime Hernandez, whose work allowed me to finally find a mirror in books and to know that other brown, nerdy, punky, tomboyish, sensitive, head-in-the-clouds girls do exist.

Sassy magazine, *Factsheet Five,* and Pander Zine Distro, without whom I might never have gotten into zines. Frank Barber, who made me my first punk mixtape. He titled the cassette *Brave New World,* and it really was. All the zines I've read and music I've listened to, including the musicians mentioned in this book, that have influenced the way I see the world and the way in which I create. All the libraries that have filled my life with books, have provided windows into other worlds, and have given me license to dream.

La Familia Perez, especially my mom and my big sister Gloria, for all their hard work and sacrifice. I bow down to you. Vicki Zeeb and the Zeeb family for love and support.

And my Perez Zeeb posse: Brett, who always believed and cheered on this book from dream to reality, Emiliano, who is my everything, and Mister Bagel too. Thank you, I love you.

There are moments when writing can feel like lonely work, but as I look back over this entire experience, the last thing I feel is alone. Mil gracias to all of you. I am honored to have you in my life.

GUATEMALAN WORRY DOLLS

According to legend, Guatemalan children tell their worries to the Worry dolls, placing them under their pillow when they go to bed at night. By morning the dolls have taken their worries away.

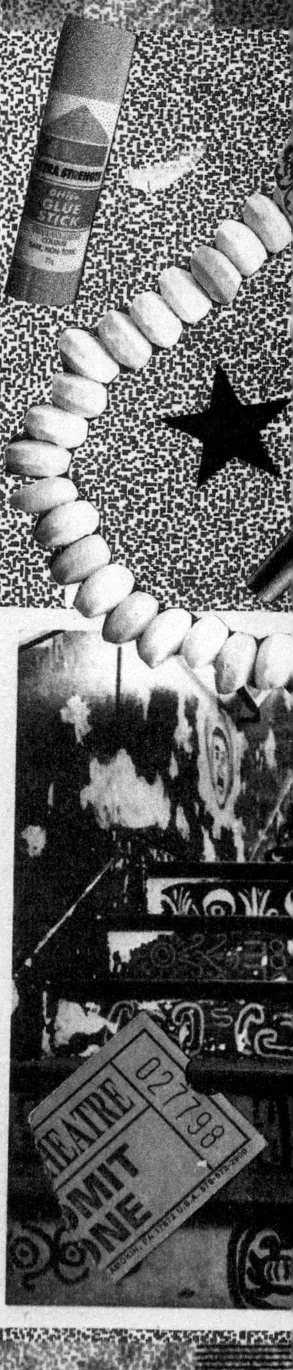

the Wolf